PUFFIN B[...]

Editor: Kay[...]

THE LITTLE MAN

His real name was Maxie Pichelsteiner but most people called him The Little Man, because he was only two inches high and slept in a matchbox. His parents were acrobats with Stilke's Circus, but they were blown off the Eiffel Tower by a sudden gust of wind when he was quite tiny, and after that Maxie was brought up by the world-famous conjurer, Professor Hokus von Pokus – along with his two doves, Minna and Emma, and his white rabbit, Alba.

The Little Man knew exactly what he was going to be when he grew up – an artiste in the circus. But the Professor was not so sure. He used to shake his head and say that Maxie was much too small, but he eventually gave in and Maxie became his apprentice. And that was the beginning of a sensational magic act that was to make Maxie more famous than the Leaning Tower of Pisa. His fame flew overnight to all the remotest corners of the globe – including, unfortunately, South America, where a sinister millionaire decided to add him to his collection of stolen rarities, and how could one tiny midget hope to outwit a private army of thieving criminal henchmen?

Erich Kästner seems to know exactly how it would feel to be only two inches high, to bath in a soap dish and ride in one's friends' pockets, so young Maxie seems just as real and lively, just as much a character as the hero in the most famous of all his books, *Emil and the Detectives*. His other books in Puffins are *Emil and the Three Twins*, *The Flying Classroom*, and *Lottie and Lisa*.

For readers of ten and over.

Erich Kästner

The Little Man

TRANSLATED FROM THE
ORIGINAL GERMAN BY
James Kirkup

ILLUSTRATED BY
Horst Lemke

PUFFIN BOOKS

Puffin Books, Penguin Books Ltd, Harmondsworth, Middlesex, England
Penguin Books Australia Ltd, Ringwood, Victoria, Australia
Penguin Books Canada Ltd, 41 Steelcase Road West,
Markham, Ontario, Canada
Penguin Books (N.Z.) Ltd, 182–190 Wairau Road,
Auckland 10, New Zealand

—

Der Kleine Mann first published by Atrium Verlag A.G., Zurich, © 1963
English translation published by Jonathan Cape 1966
Published in Puffin Books 1975

—

Translation Copyright © Jonathan Cape Ltd, 1966
Illustrations copyright © Atrium Verlag A.G., Zurich, 1963

—

Made and printed in Great Britain by
Cox & Wyman Ltd
London, Reading and Fakenham
Set in Intertype Baskerville

This book is sold subject to the condition
that it shall not, by way of trade or otherwise,
be lent, re-sold, hired out, or otherwise circulated
without the publisher's prior consent in any form of
binding or cover other than that in which it is
published and without a similar condition
including this condition being imposed
on the subsequent purchaser

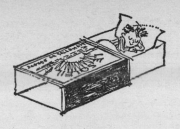

I

HE was called The Little Man and his bed was a matchbox. Actually, his real name was Maxie Pichelsteiner. But
this fact was known to very few people. And even I
wouldn't have known it if he hadn't told me so himself.
That was in London, if I remember rightly. At Garland's
Hotel. In the breakfast room, in fact, with all the pretty
birdcages hanging from the ceiling. Twitter-twitter-
twitter! One could hardly hear oneself speak.

Or was it in Rome? At the Hotel Ambassadore on the
Via Veneto? Or in the dining-room of the Hotel Excelsior
in Amsterdam? I'm afraid my memory has let me down.
Pity! Sometimes the inside of my head feels like an un-
tidied toy-cupboard.

One thing, however, is quite certain: Maxie's parents
and grandparents and great-grandparents and even his

5

great-great-great-grandparents all hailed from the most foresty part of the forests of Bohemia. There is a high mountain there, and a tiny village, both of which are named Pichelstein. I took the precaution of looking it up in my old encyclopaedia, where I found the following entry, set down in black and white:

Pichelstein. Village in Bohemia. Pop: 412. Community of very small people. Tallest height 20 inches. Causes of this unknown. Celebrated for its Amateur Gymnastics Association (Pichelstein AGA, founded 1872) and for what is known as 'Pichelstein Beef'. (For further details, see Vol. IV under entry 'Economy Dishes'.) For centuries, all inhabitants have borne the name 'Pichelsteiner'. Recommended reading: *Pichelstein and the Pichelsteiners* by the Rev. Alphonsus Funn, M.A., 1908, privately printed. O.P.

A queer sort of village, you may say. But I can't help that. The information given in my old encyclopaedia is nearly always correct.

After one year of marriage, Maxie's parents decided to set out on their travels, to seek their fortunes. Small though they were, they had big ideas. And as the village of Pichelstein in the forests of Bohemia didn't offer much scope for their plans and dreams, the pair of them set out with bag and baggage – handbag and briefcase – into the great wide world.

Everywhere they went, they caused the greatest astonishment. People's mouths dropped open and they could hardly close them again. For Maxie's mother was really as pretty as a picture, and his father sported a magnificent black moustache, yet they were no bigger than five-year-olds. No wonder people were filled with wonder!

What had Maxie's parents in mind? As they were such excellent gymnasts, they wanted to become acrobats. And

6

indeed, after they had demonstrated their stunts on the horizontal bar and on the rings before Herr Brausewetter, ringmaster of Stilke's Circus, he applauded them enthusiastically, clapping his white-kid-gloved hands and shouting: 'Bravo, you little imps! I'm signing you up!' That was in Copenhagen. At the Tivoli Gardens. One morning, it was. Inside the 'Big Top' circus tent erected on four gigantic poles. Maxie had not been born yet.

Although his parents had been leading gymnasts in Pichelstein, they still had a lot to learn, and much hard training to do. Not until three months later were they made members of the Chinese acrobatic troupe known as 'The Bamboo Family'. In fact, they were not a real family at all. And they certainly weren't real Chinese either. The twelve neatly plaited pigtails that dangled down their backs were about as genuine as forged banknotes. But as 'artistes' they were in the front rank and among the cleverest jugglers and acrobats who had ever appeared in a circus.

They would juggle with fragile cups and saucers, spinning them at the top of long, thin, flexible poles of yellow bamboo, so swiftly that the spectators could only gape in stupefaction. The younger ones would scamper like monkeys up smooth, long bamboo poles as thick as your arm, which were held upright by the biggest and strongest of the 'Chinamen'. Once at the top of the swaying poles, they would do hand-stands, and, to the accompaniment of muted drum-rolls, stand on their heads. Yes, and they would even do somersaults, a good thirty feet above the circus ring! They would flip head over heels in the air as easy as winking, and then, feet together, would stand upright on the tip of the teetering bamboo poles and smile and wave to the spectators far below. The band would give three triumphant blasts, and then the public would clap and clap until their hands were sore!

On all the posters and in the programmes Maxie's parents were now billed as Wu Fu and Chin Chin. They wore artificial pigtails and brilliantly embroidered Chinese jackets and trousers of rustling silk. They travelled

around with the rolled-up circus tent, the elephants and other wild beasts, the fire-eaters, clowns and trapeze artists, the Arabian Steeds, stable-boys, animal trainers, bare-back riders, mechanics, musicians and Herr Brausewetter, from one city to the next. They enjoyed great success, made money and thanked their lucky stars, day in day out, that they had got away from Pichelstein.

Then, in Stockholm, Maxie was born. He was so infinitely tiny that the nurse very nearly threw him away with the bathwater. Fortunately he yelled fit to raise the dead, and was saved in the nick of time. The circus doctor examined him for a long time through a magnifying glass, smiled, and finally pronounced: 'It's a boy! A fine, healthy specimen! Congratulations!'

*

When Maxie was six years old, he lost his parents. It happened in Paris, quite suddenly and unexpectedly. The couple had taken the lift up the Eiffel Tower in order to admire the beautiful view. But no sooner had they reached the topmost platform than a great gale sprang up, blew them off their feet and in a twinkling swept them up into space.

The other tourists, who were bigger, were able to cling to the metal framework of the parapet.

But it was all over with Wu Fu and Chin Chin. They were last seen, hand in hand, spinning away into the distance. Then they disappeared over the horizon.

*

Next day, the newspaper headlines ran: 'Two small Chinese swept off the Eiffel Tower! Helicopter search fails to locate them! Sad loss for Stilke's Circus!'

Of course, the loss was saddest of all for Maxie, who had loved his parents very, very much. He shed many a tiny tear into his tiny handkerchiefs.

Then a Portuguese vessel fished a pair of pigtails out of the sea, south of the Canary Islands. Two weeks later, when the two pigtails, in a single ivory coffin, were interred at the cemetery, Maxie was so overcome with grief he felt he wanted to die too.

It was a curious ceremony. All the circus folk attended the funeral: the Bamboo Family in their embroidered jackets, the lion-tamer bearing a wreath on his whip, the show rider Gallopinski on his black stallion Nero, the fire-eaters with their blazing torches, Herr Brausewetter the

9

ringmaster wearing his top-hat and white kid gloves, the clowns with sad expressions painted on their faces, and finally the person who was to deliver the grave-side oration, the world-famous illusionist, Professor Hokus von Pokus.

At the end of his solemn address, the Professor said: 'The two little colleagues we are gathered here to mourn today left their Maxie in our charge. Shortly before their ill-fated ascent of the Eiffel Tower they brought him to my hotel room and asked me to keep an eye on him until they came back. Today, alas, we know that they cannot come back. And so I must keep an eye on him as long as I live, and shall do so gladly, with all my heart. Is that all right with you, my boy?'

Maxie, who was peeping out of the breast pocket of the magician's professional tail-coat, sobbed: 'Oh yes, Hokus! It's all right with me.'

Everyone wept tears of sorrow and joy. Their tears made the make-up run on the clowns' faces. Then the Professor whipped five huge bouquets of flowers out of thin air and laid them on the tiny grave. The fire-eaters thrust their torches into their mouths, putting out the flames. The circus band struck up the 'March of the Gladiators'. And then, led by Gallopinski on his black steed Nero, they all dashed back to the circus. For it was a Wednesday.

And as everyone knows, on Wednesdays, Saturdays and Sundays there are matinee performances. For children. At reduced rates.

2

The matchbox on the bedside table.
Minna, Emma and Alba. Only two
ounces live weight, yet sound as a bell.
The Little Man wants to go to school.
Trouble in Athens and Brussels. Instruction on the folding steps. Books as small
as postage stamps.

WELL, I've already told you that at night Maxie slept in a
matchbox. Instead of the forty matches such a box nor-
mally holds, it contained a tiny cotton-wool mattress, a
small strip of camel-hair counterpane and a pillow no
larger than the nail on my middle finger. And the box was
left half-open, because otherwise the poor little chap
wouldn't have been able to breathe.

The matchbox stood on the bedside table next to the
conjurer's bed. And every night, when Professor Hokus
von Pokus had turned over to face the wall and begun to
snore softly, Maxie would switch off the bedside lamp on
the bedside table, and it would not be long before he was
asleep too.

The two doves, Minna and Emma, and Alba, the white
rabbit in his wicker basket, all slept in the same hotel room

as Maxie and the Professor. The doves would perch on the top of the wardrobe. They would hide their heads in their breast feathers, and when they dreamed they used to coo.

The three animals belonged to the Professor and helped him in his performances in the circus. The doves would suddenly flutter out of the sleeves of his tail-coat, and he would magic the rabbit out of his empty top-hat. Minna, Emma and Alba were very fond of the Professor and they were simply devoted to the little boy. After they had had breakfast at five in the morning, Maxie was even sometimes allowed to sit on Emma's back, and then she would take him for a flip round the room.

*

A matchbox is two and a quarter inches long, an inch and a half wide and three-quarters of an inch high. It was just the right size for Maxie. For even at the age of ten or twelve he only measured two inches precisely, and just fitted nicely into the box. On the hotel desk-clerk's letter-balance he weighed only two ounces, yet he always had a good appetite and had never been ill. He'd had the measles, to be sure. But the measles don't really count. Nearly every child in creation has *them*.

At the age of seven he had naturally wanted to start school. But the difficulties were all too great. For one thing, every time the circus moved on he would have had to change schools. And often even change his language, too! For in Germany the teaching was in German, in England it was in English, in France it was in French, in Italy it was in Italian and in Norway it was in Norwegian. The Little Man might well have managed even that, for he was brighter than most children of his age. But the trouble was that his classmates were all much, much

13

bigger than he, and they flattered themselves that being bigger was something special. So he had to put up with a lot, the poor chap.

In Athens, for example, during the lunch break, three little Greek girls popped him into an inkwell. And in Brussels a couple of Belgian louts stuck him on the curtain-rod. Nevertheless he climbed down again at once. Because even at that early age he could already climb better than anyone. But he had not cared for such stupid tricks at all. And so the conjurer suggested to him one day: 'Do you know what? The best thing would be for me to give you private lessons.'

'Oh, wonderful!' Maxie cried. 'That's a good idea! When do we start?'

'Tomorrow morning at nine,' replied Professor Hokus von Pokus. 'But don't start grinning too soon!'

*

It took some time before they found out the most con-venient way to arrange things. But gradually they solved their problems, and then, day by day, they began to get more and more fun from their lessons. The most import-ant things, besides the reader and the exercise-book, were a pair of folding steps and a strong magnifying-glass.

In the reading lesson, Maxie would scramble up on to the step-ladder's topmost step, because if he sat with his nose in the book the letters were too big for him. Only when he was perched on top of the steps could he read the print in comfort.

For writing, it was just the opposite. Then he had to sit at a tiny desk. The tiny desk stood on the big table. And the Professor would sit at the table and scan Maxie's scritch-scratch through the magnifying-glass. It enlarged the writing seven times, and this was the only way he could make anything at all of the letters and the words. Without the magnifying-glass, he and the bedroom waiter and the maids would have mistaken the scratchings for ink-splashes or fly-blow. And yet, as one could see quite clearly by using the magnifying-glass, the letters were prettily and delicately formed.

It was the same in the arithmetic lesson. For numbers, too, they used the steps and the magnifying-glass. And so Maxie, whether he learnt anything or not, was always on the move. Now he would be sitting on the steps, now at his desk.

One fine morning, the bedroom waiter, who had come to take away the breakfast things, remarked: 'If I didn't know for sure that the young gentleman was learning to read and write, I would certainly think he was taking lessons in gymnastics.' They all had to laugh at that. Even Minna and Emma, who were perched on the wardrobe, chortled with them. For they were chortle doves.

Maxie did not take long to learn his letters. After a very short time, he could read as fluently as if he'd been doing it all his life. And then he became, almost overnight, a bookworm. The first book that Hokus von Pokus gave him was Grimms' Fairy Tales. And quite probably he would have read them all within a week, if it had not been for those dratted folding-steps!

Every time he wanted to turn a page, there was nothing else for it but to clamber down the steps, jump down on to the table, turn the page, then scramble to the top of the steps again. That was the only way he could proceed with the story. And after reading those two pages he had to climb down again to reach the book! So this was the procedure: turn page, up steps, read two sides, down steps, on to the table, turn page quickly, up steps, read next two sides, down ladder, turn page, up – it was enough to wear one out!

One afternoon the Professor came in just as the boy was crawling up the steps for the twenty-third time, tearing his hair with rage and shouting: 'It's really awful! For heaven's sake, why aren't there any smaller books? With weeny letters?'

At first the Professor laughed at Maxie's bad temper. But then he thought a while and said: 'Really, you're quite right. And if there are no such books in existence yet, we shall have some printed for you.'

'Then is there someone who can do that?' the boy asked.

'I have no idea,' the conjurer said. 'But in March the circus will be playing Munich. Unruh, the watchmaker, lives there. We'll make inquiries of him.'

'And why would Unruh the watchmaker know?'

'I don't know if he does know. But he might well know, because he often has to do with such things. For example, ten years ago he inscribed "The Song of Hiawatha" on the back of a postage stamp. And the poem is all of four hundred and twenty-five lines in length.'

'Wow!' Maxie cried enthusiastically. 'Books no bigger than postage stamps – just the thing for me!'

In short: Unruh the watchmaker did indeed know of a printing press which could print such tiny books! All the same, it was a costly little novelty. But the Professor earned, as a conjurer, a great deal of money, and Maxie's parents had left him their savings. So it was not long before the boy had collected a pretty little library.

Now, he no longer needed to do acrobatics on the folding steps, but was able to sit down and read in comfort. He preferred reading at night, when he was lying in the matchbox, and the Professor, after falling asleep, had begun to snore softly to himself. What a cosy atmosphere! Up on the wardrobe the two doves would be cooing. And Maxie would bury himself in one of his favourite books – *Hop o' My Thumb, Nils Holgersson, Memoirs of a Midget* or, best of all, *Gulliver's Travels*.

Sometimes the Professor would mutter, half asleep: 'Turn the light out, you little wretch!'

Then Maxie would whisper: 'In a minute, Hokus.' Sometimes the 'minute' would last for half an hour. But finally he would switch the lamp off, fall asleep and dream of Gulliver in Lilliput Land, where the inhabitants looked upon him as a giant.

And this giant who strode over city walls and scuttled the enemy war-fleet was, naturally, no other than Maxie Pichelsteiner.

3

He wants to become a circus performer.
Big people and great people are not one
and the same thing. A conversation in
Strasbourg. On the profession of inter-
preter. Through Maxie's obstinacy, the
Professor's plan comes to nothing.

THE older The Little Man grew, the more often did they
discuss what he should be. Each time he would declare: 'I
want to enter the circus. I want to become an artiste.' And
each time the Professor would shake his head and say:
'But my dear boy, that wouldn't do at all! You're much
too small for it!'

'Sometimes you say one thing, sometimes another,'
Maxie grumbled. 'You're always telling me how many
famous men were small: Napoleon and Julius Caesar and
Goethe and Einstein and a dozen others. You also told me
that tall people are very seldom great people! Their
strength goes to seed, you said, and when they are six feet
tall it doesn't leave much over for their brains.'

The Professor scratched his head. Finally he declared:

'Anyhow, Caesar and Napoleon and Goethe and Einstein would not have made good circus performers. Caesar's legs were so short, he could hardly sit on a horse!'

'I have not the slightest desire to sit on a horse,' the boy retorted irritably. 'Were my parents bad artistes?'

'Far from it! They were first class.'

'And were they tall?'

'No, on the contrary, they were very small.'

'Well then, my dear Hokus?'

'There's no "well then" about it,' the conjurer said. 'They were small, but you are ten times smaller. You are too small! If you were standing in the ring, the public would simply not see you!'

'Then they'd have to bring opera-glasses with them,' The Little Man declared.

'Do you know what you are?' Hokus asked grimly. 'You are a big numskull.'

'No, I'm a little numskull, and . . .'

'And?' the Professor asked eagerly.

'And I shall become an artiste!' Maxie cried, so loudly that Alba the white rabbit let the lettuce-leaf he was nibbling drop from his jaws with the shock.

*

One evening after the circus performance they were sitting in the restaurant of an hotel in Strasbourg, and Professor Hokus von Pokus was enjoying some truffled goose-liver pâté. He nearly always ate after the performance, because if he ate before it, his tail-coat became too tight. And that interfered with his magicking.

For he concealed all kinds of things in his tail-coat. For example, four packs of cards, five bunches of flowers, twenty razor blades and eight lighted cigarettes. Besides these, the doves Minna and Emma, the white rabbit Alba

and everything else he needed for his conjuring tricks. With all that, it's better to dine later.

So now he was sitting at the table eating Strasbourg goose-liver pâté and toast, and Maxie was sitting up on the table right next to the plate, letting himself be fed with tiny morsels. Then there was a Wiener Schnitzel, fruit salad and black coffee. The Little Man even got a sip of the coffee. Finally they were full and satisfied and stretched their legs out in front of them, the Professor's under the table and The Little Man's on the table.

'I know now what you'll be,' Hokus said, after blowing a wonderfully pretty white ring of cigarette smoke.

Maxie gazed in admiration at the smoke-ring, which grew ever bigger and thinner until it was hovering round the chandelier. Then he said: 'Have you just found it out now? I've known all along. I'm going to be an artiste.'

'No,' growled the Professor. 'You're going to be an interpreter!'

'An interpreter?'

'It's a very interesting occupation. You can already speak German and quite a lot of English and French and a bit of Italian and Spanish and ...'

'Dutch and Swedish and Danish,' The Little Man went on.

'Quite, quite,' the Professor broke in hurriedly. 'When we've traipsed round Europe with the circus for another couple of years you'll be able to speak all those languages even better. Then you'll sit an examination in Geneva, at the famous Interpreters' School. And as soon as you've passed it, we'll set off for Bonn. A good friend of mine lives there.'

'Is he a conjurer too?'

'No, he's something much better. He is a Government employee. He is Chief Information Officer in the Federal Chancellery. I'll show him your Geneva diploma, and then, if all goes well, you'll become interpreter for the Foreign Office or even for the Federal Chancellor himself. He is the most important and powerful of all. And as he is often abroad and has to talk to other Chancellors, he needs a really good interpreter.'

'But not a Tom Thumb!'

'On the contrary,' the Professor retorted. 'The smaller the better! For example, he takes you to Paris, because he has to talk about something with the French President. Something very top-secret. Something frightfully important. But because the German Chancellor can't speak French very well, he needs a translator who can explain to him what the French President is saying.'

'And he has to ask me, of all people?'

'Yes, indeed, my Little Man,' the Professor went on. He

21

was very much taken with his idea. 'You sit yourself in the Chancellor's ear and whisper to him in German whatever the President says in French.'

'But I'll always be tumbling down,' Maxie said.

'No. In the first place, perhaps he has such huge ears that you can sit right inside.'

'And in the second place? What if he has only very tiny ears?'

'Then he'll hang a fine gold chain round his ear-lobe, you'll seat yourself on the chain, become known as Counsellor Extraordinary Maxie Pichelsteiner and people will refer to you with bated breath as "the official who has the Chancellor's ear". Wouldn't that be nice?'

'No!' Maxie cried loudly. 'I should find it horrible! I won't be any Little Man in anyone's ear. Neither in Germany nor in France nor at the North Pole. You've forgotten the main thing.'

'And what is the main thing?'

'I'm going to be an artiste.'

4

The Little Man wants to become a lion-tamer. Lions are cats, aren't they? Adventure with minced meat and whip. Maxie in the tooth-glass. Report of an extraordinary game of football. Hokus jumps through a flaming hoop.

WHEN the Stilke Circus was once more playing in Milan, Maxie said, on the third day, quite excited: 'Hokus, listen, the hotel cat's got kittens. Four of them. They're eight weeks old and in Room 228 they're jumping from the chairs to the table, then when they're on the table they jump down again.'

'Well now,' the Professor said, 'I think that's very sensible of them. They couldn't stay on the table for ever!'

But today The Little Man was in no mood for jokes. 'The maids showed them to me,' he went on eagerly. 'They are striped, and look just like little tigers.'

'Did they scratch you?'

'Not at all,' the boy assured him. 'In fact, we got on very nicely together. They were purring, and I fed them with some minced meat.'

23

The Professor looked at him out of the corner of his eye. Then he asked: 'What are you cooking up? Eh? What have you got up your sleeve? Out with it!'

Maxie took a deep breath and, after a pause, declared: 'I'm going to train them and present them in the circus.'

'Who, the maids?'

'No!' the boy cried in exasperation. 'The kittens!'

Taken aback, Hokus von Pokus sat down on the chair and was silent for two or three minutes. Finally he shook his head, sighed and said: 'It is impossible to train cats. I thought you knew that.'

Maxie smiled confidently and then asked: 'Aren't lions cats?'

'Yes, yes. They belong to the hunting cats. You're quite correct there.'

'And tigers? And leopards?'

'They are also hunters, members of the great cat family. Quite correct again.'

'When the tamer commands don't they sit on high pedestals? Don't they jump through hoops?'

'Even through flaming hoops,' the Professor agreed.

The boy rubbed his hands gleefully. 'There you are!' he cried, triumphantly. 'If it's possible to train such big cats, it should be all the more possible to train kittens.'

'No!' the Professor firmly stated. 'It's quite impossible!'

'And why not?'

'I have no idea.'

'But *I* know the reason,' Maxie declared haughtily.

'Well?'

'Because no one has tried it yet!'

'And you want to try?'

'I do. I've already thought of a name for the number. The posters will read: "Maxie and His Four Kittens,

Breath-Taking Animal-Training Act, Presented for the First Time!" Perhaps I'll appear wearing a black mask. And I'll also need a whip to crack. But I have one already. I'll use the whip from my old toy stage-coach.'

'Well, I wish you joy, my young friend,' Hokus von Pokus said, and opened his newspaper.

*

The very next morning the maids put four low stools in Room 228. The four little kittens sniffed inquisitively round the stools, but soon toddled back to their basket and rolled themselves up in a sleepy ball.

Then the floor waiter appeared. In his left hand he was carrying a plate and in his right hand he held Maxie, who was holding in *his* right hand the lacquered toy whip and in his left hand a sharp toothpick. 'To keep the wild beasts at bay,' he explained. 'Just in case they should attack the trainer. And to stick the meat on.'

'Shall I stay with you?' the friendly waiter asked.

'No, thank you,' The Little Man replied. 'That would interfere with the training. It would distract the animals.'

So the waiter went away. The trainer was left alone with his four victims. They blinked their eyes at him, yawned soundlessly, stretched, and began to lick each other as if they hadn't washed for a week.

'Now listen and get this straight,' the boy shouted sharply. 'This lazy life has got to stop. From today, you're going to work. Is that clear?'

They went on washing each other and behaved as if they were hard of hearing. He gave a whistle. He clicked his tongue. He stuck the lacquer whip under his arm and snapped his fingers. He stuck the toothpick under the other arm and clapped his hands. He cracked his whip.

He stamped his foot. The cats didn't even prick up their ears.

Only when Maxie, using the toothpick, had manoeuvred a few bits of meat on to the footstools did the four come to life. They hopped out of the basket, jumped on the stools, gobbled up the bits of meat, licked their lips and gazed expectantly at their trainer.

'That's the way,' he cried enthusiastically. 'Bravo! Now you must sit up and beg. Alley-oop! Fore-paws in the air!' He pointed upwards with his whip.

But the kittens must have misunderstood him. Or else they'd smelt that there was more chopped meat in Room 228. Anyhow, they dived off the stools, made a bee-line for the dish and began tucking in as if they were on the brink of starvation.

'No!' yelled The Little Man, infuriated. 'Leave that alone! This minute! Can't you hear what I'm saying?'

They couldn't hear. Even if they had wanted to. And they didn't want to in the least. They lapped at the dish till it shook.

Maxie was shaking even more. But he was shaking with rage.

'You get your chopped meat afterwards! First you must stand on your hind legs! And march in single file! And jump from one stool to the next! D'you understand?' He rapped the dish with his whip.

Then one of the cats snatched the pretty lacquered whip away from him and bit it in two!

*

As Professor Hokus von Pokus, deep in thought, was coming along the hotel corridor, he heard squeals for help coming from Room 228. He threw the door open, looked about him and began to laugh.

26

The four cats were sitting under the wash-basin, gazing excitedly in the air. Their little whiskers were bristling. Their little tails were beating the floor. And up above, on the edge of the wash-basin, Maxie was crouched in a tooth-glass, weeping. 'Help me, Hokus!' he called. 'They want to gobble me up!'

'What nonsense!' the Professor retorted. 'You're not made of minced meat, after all. And you're not a mouse either.' Then he fished the boy out of the tooth-glass and examined him thoroughly, back, front and sides. 'Your clothes are a little torn, and you have a scratch on your left cheek. That's all.'

'What a lot of hooligans!' Maxie complained. 'First they broke my whip and chewed the toothpick to pieces, and then they played football!'

'Football? With what?'

'With me! Oh, Hokus, they tossed me in the air and caught me again and shot me under the bed and hauled me out again and dribbled me over the parquet and then booted me into the air again and shot me under the bed again and pulled me out and bundled me under the carpet and fished me out again, it was frightful! If I hadn't caught hold of the towel and clambered up to the wash-basin and into the tooth-glass, heaven knows if I'd be alive now to tell the tale!'

'Poor old chap,' the Professor said. 'But it's all over now. I'll bath you and put you to bed.'

The four kittens blinked spitefully at the Professor. They were vexed that the big man had taken away their little football that gave such splendid screams when they played with it. Then they stretched their hind legs, trotted over to the dish and stuck their noses in it. But the dish had been well and truly licked clean.

The smartest of the four thought: 'Too bad!' and curled up like a pretzel on the bedside rug. Just before he dropped off, he thought: 'I can only eat when someone brings something. Sleeping is easier. Because I don't need anyone to do that.'

*

Meanwhile Maxie was sitting woebegone in his match-box, with sticking-plaster on his cheek, drinking hot chocolate out of his wee little Meissen porcelain cup.

The Professor had stuck a watchmaker's glass in his eye and was mending the rents in Maxie's clothes.

'So you're quite positive one can't train cats?' The Little Man asked.

'Quite positive.'

'Are they more stupid than lions and tigers?'

'No question of it,' the Professor said decisively. 'They

28

simply don't enjoy it. I can well understand why. *I* wouldn't enjoy jumping through flaming hoops either.'

Maxie couldn't help laughing. 'That's a real shame! Just imagine! Only animals for spectators. Kangaroos and bears and sea-lions and horses and pelicans. Just think of that! All seats sold out!' He was so pleased with himself, he tugged at his hair and shouted: 'There! Now make up the next part of the story.'

'Very well,' said the Professor. 'In the orchestra-box, the elephants blow a trumpet blast. Then the lion enters the ring. He has a whip in his paw and a top-hat on his golden mane. There is dead quiet suddenly. Four solemn tigers drag a cage into the ring. Inside the cage sits a man in a tail-coat, growling.'

'Marvellous!' Maxie rubbed his hands. 'And the man is *you*!'

'That's right. The lion sweeps off his top-hat with a flourish, bows and cries: "And now, ladies and gentlemen of the animal kingdom, we have the great attraction on our programme! I have succeeded in taming a man. He is a very well educated person. His name is Professor Hokus von Pokus. Before your very eyes, ladies and gentlemen, he will jump through a flaming paper hoop! I beg the woodpeckers in the band to favour us with a muted drum-roll!" The woodpeckers begin drumming. The cage opens. Two tigers hold a hoop in the air. The lion cracks his whip. I emerge slowly from the cage, and snarl. The lion cracks his whip again. I climb on the pedestal and snarl again. A glow-worm sets the hoop on fire. It begins to flame. With a flick of his whip, the lion lashes the seat of my trousers. I roar with rage. He lashes me again. And then, with one great lunge, I leap through the blazing hoop. The paper bursts. The flames dance. I've done it! The elephants trumpet. The woodpeckers drum. I get up off the sand, dust my trousers and give a deep bow.'

'And all the animals in the circus clap like mad,' The Little Man cried excitedly, 'and the lion rewards you with a veal cutlet!'

'And now you're going to sleep, young man,' the Professor ordered. He looked at his wrist-watch. 'It's Wednesday, and I must go for the afternoon performance.'

'Happy conjuring!' said Maxie. 'But there's just one thing more.'

'What's that?'

'Nothing could be done, unfortunately, with the four cats.'

'No.'

'But one thing's quite certain. I'm going to be an artiste.'

5

A window-shopping expedition and a
tailor's dummy. The shop assistant
faints. After all, a gentlemen's outfitter's
is not a hospital. The difference between
a statesman and a milkman.

ONE hot day in July the pair were strolling leisurely
through the West End of Berlin, looking at the window
displays. Actually, it was only the Professor who was walking. Maxie was not strolling at all, but was standing in the
breast pocket of the Professor's jacket. He had propped
his arms on the edge of the pocket, as if the pocket were a
balcony, and showed especial interest in the windows of
toyshops, delicatessens and bookshops. But things didn't
always go to his liking. The Professor also enjoyed looking
at displays of shoes, shirts, ties, cigars, umbrellas, wines
and everything under the sun.

'Don't keep standing such a long time in front of this
chemist's,' the boy pleaded. 'Let us walk on.'

'Us?' Hokus asked. 'What do you mean – us? To the
best of my knowledge, only one of us is walking, and that
is I. Are *you* walking? No sign of it, old chap. You are not

walking. You are being walked. I've got you well in hand.'

'You haven't,' the little imp retorted. 'You have me in your pocket!'

They couldn't help laughing at that. And people turned round to stare. A plump Berliner nudged his wife and murmured: 'There's a funny thing, Rieke! That man's laughing with two voices.'

'Well, let him have his little joke!' Rieke replied. 'Perhaps he's a ventriloquist.'

*

Again the Professor stopped for rather a long time outside a window displaying gentlemen's wear. He looked at the tailor's dummies in their fine suits, walked on a few steps, turned back, examined the window display again, fell into deep thought, gave three vigorous nods and said to himself out loud: 'That's not such a silly idea!'

'What isn't such a silly idea?' Maxie asked, curious.

However, the Professor did not reply, but strode right away into the shop and told the dapper assistant, before the latter could open his mouth: 'I'd like the navy-blue suit in the window. The single-breasted one at two hundred and ninety-five marks.'

'Very well, sir. But I don't think it will fit you.'

'That doesn't matter,' the Professor murmured.

'Perhaps a few alterations may be necessary,' the assistant suggested politely. 'I'll ask the tailor to come down from the workshop.'

'He needn't bother.'

'It will take only a short time, sir.'

'If he doesn't come down, it will take even less.'

'But our firm sets great store on giving its customers satisfaction,' the assistant remarked, slightly nettled.

'That's very creditable,' the Professor said. 'But I don't want to wear your navy-blue suit. I just want to buy it!'

'In that case I would advise that the gentleman for whom the suit is intended should kindly pay us a visit,' the assistant suggested. 'Or if you would give us his address, we would send our tailor to his house. We can do it this very afternoon.' He pulled out his notebook in order to write down the address.

The Professor shook his head violently. 'Your navy-blue suit out there in the window is intended neither for myself nor for any other living creature.'

The assistant turned pale and retreated a step. Then he moaned: 'Not for any living creature, sir? Then it's for – for a dead man? Oh!' He drew a deep breath and went on: 'May I ask for the measurements of the – the dear departed? Even for a dead man, the suit must fit, more or less. Or else one of our tailors could be . . .'

'Nonsense!' the Professor answered brusquely. Then he calmed down again. 'Naturally, you don't know what it's all about.'

'It would appear so,' admitted the assistant, completely frightened by now. He was holding on tightly to the counter, because his knees were knocking. The poor fellow was shaking like a jelly.

'The important thing is that the suit fits your display dummy. It does, doesn't it?'

'Of course, sir.'

'What I want is to buy the suit *and* the dummy,' the Professor explained. 'Without the dummy wearing it, the suit is of no interest to me.'

Before the assistant had time to recover a little, a small voice piped up which he had not heard until then: 'But why do you need the big dummy with the blond moustache?'

The assistant gaped thunderstruck at his queer customer's breast pocket. Maxie nodded amiably at the man and said: 'Please don't be alarmed!'

'But . . .' the assistant whimpered. 'First a suit for a dead man along with the dummy in the window, and now a little imp in the jacket pock – . . . it's too much!' He rolled his eyes and collapsed on the carpet.

'Is he dead?' the boy asked.

'No, he's only fainted,' Hokus answered, and beckoned to the manager.

'And what do we really need a tailor's dummy for?' the little fellow asked.

'I'll tell you later,' said Hokus.

After the manager had hurried up and hoisted his assistant on a chair to give him a chance to regain consciousness, the Professor again made his wishes known. 'I should like to buy the navy-blue single-breasted suit, along with the dummy wearing it. Also the shirt he has on, the tie, the braces, the shoes and the socks. How much is all that, please?'

The manager replied, unsteadily: 'I don't know exactly, sir.'

The assistant moved his pallid lips and stammered out: 'Five hundred and twelve marks. One per cent discount for cash payment. Comes to five hundred and six marks, eighty-eight pfennigs.' It was obvious he was a most capable assistant. Then he slithered off his chair.

'He's fainted again,' declared Maxie, matter-of-factly.

When the manager heard the new voice and saw the little boy in the breast pocket, he squinted and grabbed desperately at the back of the chair.

'Is that gentleman going to faint as well?' Maxie inquired hopefully.

'It's to be hoped not,' the Professor said. 'After all, a gentlemen's outfitters is not a hospital.'

*

Well, the manager and his assistant recovered. The purchase was made. A taxi was summoned. The car's roof was slid back, and, held by the Professor, the tailor's dummy stood upright in the vehicle.

'That fellow looks like a foreign statesman on a state visit!' cried one Berliner as the taxi drove past.

'He can't be a statesman,' another declared.

'How's that?' the former asked. 'Who else would stand up in a car, as if it hadn't any seats?'

'He's definitely no statesman,' the other repeated obstinately. 'He's not smiling, and he hasn't waved at us once. But he would have to do those things if he were a statesman. He would have to show how tremendously pleased he was to be in Berlin and unable to sit down. Otherwise he's no statesman.'

The car stopped at a crossing and the two Berliners trotted over towards it. But before they reached it, the lights turned green and they were left standing.

'Besides, no statesman ever travels in a common taxi,' one of the men said, 'either sitting or standing.'

'I've never had a ride in a taxi,' the other said.

'Well, then, me old cock, you can't be a statesman!'

'No, I'm a milkman.'

6

Agitation at the Hotel Kempinski. Herr Hinkeldey suddenly misses all kinds of things, gets them back again and takes to his heels. What was Hokus before he became a conjurer? And why did he buy the display dummy?

AT the Hotel Kempinski, too, where Professor Hokus von Pokus was staying, many eyebrows were raised. The staff there had gradually got used to The Little Man who slept on the bedside table in a matchbox. But the hotel manager and the doorman became distinctly nervous when they saw a tailor's dummy being carried by two hotel porters through the astonished lobby of the hotel.

Hardly had the dummy been set down in the middle of the room than the manager burst in, gazed reproachfully through his horn-rimmed glasses and demanded to know the meaning of all this.

'The meaning of all what?' the Professor replied amiably, as if he couldn't understand what all the excitement was about.

'The display dummy.'

'I need it for professional purposes,' Hokus explained. 'Concert pianists and singers bring even their own grand pianos into the hotel with them when they are on a concert tour, and play and make all kinds of noise for hours on end. They are artists and have to practise. I am a conjurer. I too must practise! And I don't make nearly as much uproar as my musical colleagues.' He took hold of the manager's jacket and slapped him jovially on the shoulder. 'What are you so concerned about, my dear fellow?'

'It's all getting too much for us!' the manager groaned. 'Your Maxie and the two doves and the white rabbit and now this wooden doll in a blue suit . . .'

In a fatherly manner, the Professor pressed the utterly demoralized gentleman to his breast and consolingly smoothed his hair. 'Don't take it so tragically! My dummy requires no bed. He needs no towels. He won't burn the tablecloth with cigarettes. He won't bawl at the maids . . .'

'That's all very well, Herr Professor,' the manager agreed. 'But after all, you only booked a single room. And now you are living in it with The Little Man and three animals and a tailor's dummy. That makes, all told, five persons!'

'Oh, so that's the way the wind's blowing,' the conjurer said, smiling. 'Would you agree to the overcrowding of your charming room with the southern outlook if I paid you five extra marks a day?'

'That sounds reasonable,' the manager replied hesitantly. 'May I convey your esteemed offer to our cashier?'

'You may,' the Professor replied, and added, warmly shaking the man's hand: 'You'd better make a note of it at once. Here is my fountain pen.'

'Thank you very much, I have a ball-point pen and

notebook on me always. They are part of my job. They are my tools, in a sense.' The manager's hand dived into his jacket. He searched and searched and could find nothing. 'Extraordinary!' he muttered. 'No notebook! No ball-point pen! Yet I can't have left them in my office. It would be the first time in my life I'd done so.' And he went on searching his pockets. Suddenly he turned as white as a sheet and whispered: 'My wallet's missing too! There was a whole wad of money in it.'

'Now calm down,' said Hokus. 'You'd best sit down and smoke a cigarette. You may offer me one too. I feel like a smoke.'

'With pleasure,' the manager said, and immediately felt in his right pocket. Then in the left. Then in his trouser pockets. His face grew longer and longer. 'I've forgotten that too,' he stammered. 'My cigarette case. And my gold lighter, both missing . . .'

'Allow me,' the Professor said, and brought out a cigarette case and a gold lighter.

The manager looked at the Professor in bewilderment.

'What's the matter? Have you lost something else?'

'Please forgive me for suggesting it,' the manager said jerkily, 'but might it not be possible that that cigarette case and lighter do not belong to you at all, Herr Professor, but to me?'

Hokus looked closely at the two objects and said in perplexity: 'Really?'

'My monogram should be engraved on the case, a G and an H. Gustav Hinkeldey. That happens to be my name.'

'A G and an H?' the Professor said, examining the case. 'That's right, Herr Hinkeldey.' He immediately returned the objects.

'I must really beg your pardon for making so bold as to

38

draw your attention to . . .' the manager began, in some confusion.

'Not at all, not at all, Herr Hinkeldey. If either of us is to blame, it is I. So please excuse me — you know, sometimes I'm so absent-minded, I put in my pockets things which don't belong to me at all.' The Professor cautiously patted his pockets. 'Why, there's something else here!' he exclaimed in astonishment, and produced a notebook and a ball-point pen. 'Perhaps these things are yours too?'

'Yes, indeed!' Herr Hinkeldy said eagerly, and snatched them both. 'I just couldn't understand how I didn't have my notebook with me.' Then he fell silent and thoughtful, until finally he asked, suspiciously, 'In your absent-mindedness, did you also, perhaps, slip my wallet into your pocket?'

'I should very much hope not!' the Professor replied, feeling himself all over. 'Or can this be it here?' He waved in his left hand a black morocco leather wallet.

'Yes, it is!' the manager shouted, grabbed it and ran for the door at top speed, as if he were afraid the wallet might disappear again.

'Is the money still inside?' Hokus asked, highly amused.

'Yes.'

'Please, count the notes! I should not like you to complain later that some of them are missing. Put on your horn-rimmed glasses and count it all carefully!'

'My glasses? I've already got them on,' Herr Hinkeldey said.

Only when The Little Man began to laugh, and went on laughing ever more loudly and heartily, did Hinkeldey start, grab at the bridge of his nose and then let his hand drop in perplexity. 'Where have they disappeared to?'

'Now, where does one put one's spectacles when one

takes them off without thinking?' the Professor asked helpfully. 'I wouldn't know. Because I myself have never worn spectacles in my life. Have you got them in your case?'

The Little Man was almost choking with laughter. 'Stop it, Hokus!' he cried ecstatically. 'I can't bear any more. I'd fall out of your breast pocket with laughing.'

The manager gave him a scowl. 'What's so funny?' he growled. Suddenly it dawned on him: his spectacles were on the Professor's nose! With one movement he sprang back to the middle of the room, snatched the spectacles, rushed back to the door and yelled: 'You're a proper devil!'

'No, he's a conjurer, Herr Hinkeldey.'

But the manager was in no mood for any more. Not even for a little conversation. He flung open the door and shook the dust of the room from his feet. (Although in such well-kept hotels as this, there is no dust lying about anywhere.)

*

After Maxie had somewhat recovered from this joke, he said admiringly: 'Herr Hinkeldey is quite right: You're a proper devil. I've seen you at it often enough in the circus, when you bring two or even three people out of the audience and empty their pockets without their noticing a thing.'

'One simply has to keep on talking to them nicely,' Hokus said. 'One has to keep patting them on the shoulder in a friendly way. One has to buttonhole them. One has to pretend to be brushing a shred of tobacco or a piece of thread from their clothes. The rest is not all that difficult once one has learned how.'

'And how did you learn? And where? Just hold me up

against your ear a moment, will you? I must ask you something very, very softly.'

The Professor carefully extracted The Little Man from his breast pocket and held him to his ear.

'Dear Hokus,' Maxie whispered, 'you can trust me. I'll definitely not let it go any further. Were you perhaps, earlier in your life, a pickpocket?'

'No,' the Professor gently answered. 'No, Maxie mine.' He smiled and gave the little chap a kiss on the tip of the nose, and that was no easy matter. 'I was no pickpocket. But I caught many pickpockets.'

'Oh!'

'And so I had to learn to do at least as much as they could.'

'Yes, yes. Naturally. But for whom did you catch them?'

'For the police.'

'Good heavens!'

'You're surprised, eh? When I was a young man I wanted to become a detective or a criminal investigator. And later become frightfully famous.'

'Go on,' Maxie begged.

'Not now. Perhaps some other time. Today I'll tell you something about the display dummy we've bought.'

'I'd very nearly forgotten him.'

'You'll have plenty of opportunities to remember him,' the Professor said, 'because we bought him on your account.'

'On my account? What for?'

'Well, because you're so set on becoming an artiste.'

The Little Man stared at him in surprise. 'And we need the big dummy for that? Then what kind of artiste am I to be?'

'You're to be the conjurer's apprentice,' said the conjurer.

7

On bakers' apprentices, butchers' apprentices, pineapple tarts and conjurers' apprentices. The doll is named Waldemar Blockhead. Hokus outlines the course of instruction, and The Little Man is shocked. The song of 'The Invisible Right-Hand Man'.

So now The Little Man was a conjurer's apprentice, and naturally he was very pleased. But he would have been even more pleased if he had known what a conjurer's apprentice really was. 'I know what a baker's apprentice is,' he said. 'A baker's apprentice must learn the trade of a master-baker. He must learn how to bake bread and rolls and apple-pie and pineapple tarts.'

'Correct,' the Professor said.

'And a butcher's apprentice must learn how to kill pigs and to make all kinds of sausages and jellied meats.'

'That's right.'

'And if one has been a good apprentice, one is promoted to assistant. Some day shall I perhaps be a conjurer's assistant?'

42

'That's not altogether unlikely.'

'And if I . . .' Maxie began.

'Stop!' the Professor cried. 'Do you want to be a master-conjurer too?'

The Little Man shook his head. 'The world would seem a much better place, dear Hokus, if I were to be treated, right now, to a pineapple tart.'

'You're a spoilt little devil,' the Professor said, but went to the telephone, ordered a pineapple tart, and, for himself, a cognac. Then he sat in a chintzy armchair and declared: 'It's a tricky business. A baker's apprentice learns whatever the master-baker can teach him. The plumber's apprentice learns whatever the master-plumber can teach him.'

'And the butcher's apprentice . . .'

'We'll leave him out of it.'

'Oh, but why?' asked Maxie.

'Because if we do you'll get an appetite for sausage,' Hokus answered. 'Let's go no further than the plumbers.'

'All right. So I must learn from you whatever you can teach me,' The Little Man said. 'But that won't do at all. How on earth can I learn to swallow twenty big razor blades and then pull them, all strung on a thread, back out of my mouth? And after all, I can't produce a rabbit from a top hat! The sort of tiny rabbits I would need exist only in Lilliput, and Lilliput simply doesn't exist! And your playing-cards and magic wand and bouquets of flowers and lighted cigarettes – all these are at least twenty times too big for me.'

The Professor nodded. 'I've already told you it's a tricky business. All apprentices learn what their masters know: the baker's apprentice, the plumber's apprentice, the tailor's apprentice, the shoemaker's apprentice . . .'

43

'... the butcher's apprentice,' Maxie added, giggling.

'Yes, he too,' Hokus agreed. 'But you are the only apprentice in the world who has to learn what his master does not know.'

'What do you mean? You can do everything!'

'Can I sleep in a matchbox? Can I fly round the room on Minna the dove's back?'

'No. You're quite right. You can't.'

'Or can I,' went on the Professor, 'peep out of my breast pocket? Can I climb on the curtain-rail? Can I crawl through the keyhole?'

'No, you can't do those things either. Gracious, the things you *can't* do! Oh, that's a good one, Hokus!'

'Whether it's a good one or not,' the Professor declared, 'things are as they are. You are the conjurer's apprentice, I am the master, and with my help you shall learn a few things that I myself cannot do.'

At this point they were interrupted. For the waiter entered the room. He brought in the cognac and the pineapple tart. And very nearly knocked over the display dummy in the process. 'Well, I never!' he cried. 'Who on earth's this?'

'This is Winsome Waldemar,' Hokus explained. 'One of our distant relatives.'

'A very pretty gentleman,' the waiter declared, and winked at them gaily. 'Has he a surname too?'

'He's called Blockhead,' The Little Man said, keeping an utterly straight face. 'Waldemar Blockhead.'

'You meet all sorts in these big hotels,' the waiter said. Then he bowed to the display dummy, greeted him with: 'A pleasant stay in Berlin, Herr Blockhead, sir!' and went out.

After the Professor had drunk his cognac and Maxie

44

had demolished with his wee silver cake-fork a tenth part of the pineapple tart, the conjurer's apprentice began his lessons.

'You watched just now how I secretly appropriated a few objects belonging to the manager,' the Professor said.

'I watched all right,' The Little Man answered. 'But I didn't *see* anything. Not even the smart trick with the spectacles. I only noticed it when you already had them on your own nose.'

'Would you like to know how I learnt that trick? I was once an apprentice myself, you know, and had to practise a long, long time.'

'But how?'

'On a doll in a blue suit.'

'Really? And did he look as handsome as Waldemar?'

'Waldemar is handsomer and blonder,' the Professor had to admit. 'But we won't allow ourselves to be distracted by his staggering good looks. Anyhow, when you've been climbing all over him day after day, perhaps you'll no longer find him quite so attractive.'

'What have I to do?' Maxie asked, startled. 'Climb all over him for hours and hours every day?'

'Yes, indeed, my boy. From his shirt collar to the soles of his shoes, and from the soles of his shoes to his necktie. From top to bottom and from bottom to top, *into* all his pockets and *out* of all his pockets, nimble as a squirrel and soft as an ant in slippers – oh, you'll soon learn. You Pichelsteiners are after all celebrated gymnasts.'

'And what, dear Hokus, is the point of my learning all this?'

'So that you can be a competent assistant to me in the circus. I shall be able to magic away many more things

45

than before from the respected ladies and gentlemen whom I invite into the ring.'

'Then you and I, no, then me and you, no then *we'll* both be a band of thieves!'

'That's right.'

'You'll be the robber chief. And what shall I be?'

'You'll be The Invisible Right-Hand Man.'

The Little Man rubbed his hands. He often did that when he was pleased. 'That's like a cue for a song!' he cried. And he began to sing right away: 'The Invisible Right-Hand Man, ha-ha ... I climb all over Waldemar.'

'Go on.'

'It's your turn now.'

'All right, then,' said the Professor, and sang: 'I conjure with Professor Hokus ... in the circus ...'

'Hokus-Pokus!' yelled Maxie. 'Now once more all together! And frightfully loud, both of us at the same time!'

The Professor raised his hands like the conductor of a male-voice choir, gave the sign to begin, and they sang with all their might:

> 'The Invisible Right-Hand Man, ha-ha,
> I climb all over Waldemar.
> I conjure with Professor Hokus
> In the circus, Hokus-Pokus!'

The Little Man clapped excitedly. 'Please, let's sing it again, three or four times at least! It's a wonderful song.'

They sang it till the waiter knocked, came into the room and inquired anxiously whether either of them or possibly both of them felt unwell.

'We're hale and hearty,' The Little Man cried.

'We're just being silly,' the Professor added.

They sang the song to him slowly, and then the waiter sang it with them.

Then the maid came in. She was even more concerned about them than the waiter had been. But she was soon reassured. Finally the four of them were singing in chorus. It sounded like an evening of community songs. Though not quite as nice.

*

That evening, as he lay in his matchbox, Maxie yawned, stretched himself and said: 'So today was my first lesson.'

'And the easiest,' the Professor added. 'From tomorrow morning we'll start working in earnest. Put the light out, Invisible Right-Hand Man!'

'Aye, aye, Robber Captain, sir!' Maxie switched the light off. The moon shone through the window. Winsome Waldemar was standing in the middle of the room, asleep on his feet. Minna and Emma, the two doves, were perched peacefully on his wooden head. It was not as comfortable as on the wardrobe, but it did make a change.

The Professor gave his first snore. The Little Man hummed softly to himself: 'I conjure with Professor Hokus, in the circus, Hokus-Pokus!' And then his eyes closed in sleep.

8

Hokus is an outsider. Maxie in the role
of 'Maxie the Mountaineer'. The mixed-
up tail-coats. The Three Marzipan
Sisters. What is a trampoline? Gallopinski conjures on horseback. Hokus von
Pokus refuses to perform.

THEY trained for several hours every morning. Afterwards The Little Man would take a bath in the soap-dish.
They trained in all the cities where the Stilke Circus
played. When they were travelling the display dummy
Waldemar would lie in the luggage rack of their com-
partment, and they were careful to see that he did not fall
down.

They did not travel with the numerous circus wagons
which were coupled to one or more goods trains: the caravans; the horse-boxes and wild-animal cages; the wagons
carrying the Big Top, the wiring for the thousands of
electric lights, the musical instruments, the heating equipment, the trapezes and tight-ropes, the posters and sign-
boards, the costumes and carpets and seats and steps and
pay-boxes and animal attendants and cashiers and workmen and workmen's tools and the hay and the straw.

Nor did they travel with Brausewetter the ringmaster, with his top-hat and his wife, his four daughters and two sons and the sons-in-law and daughters-in-law and the seven grandchildren and the – now I really seem to have lost the thread – what was it I was trying to say, in fact?

Ah, yes, I remember. They did not travel with the circus, but took express trains. And they did not live in caravans, but in hotel rooms. The Professor was, as he said, a born outsider. 'I love the circus very much,' he said. 'But only when it's filled with people. Otherwise I prefer an ordinary life and fine weather.'

'And me!' Maxie cried as loudly as he could.

'I like *you*,' said Hokus tenderly, 'one-quarter of an inch more than fine weather.'

For half a year now The Little Man had been clambering about Winsome Waldemar like a mountaineer in the Dolomites or in the Swiss Alps, except that he was not roped. This was dangerous. For to him the tailor's dummy was as big as a skyscraper is to us.

Fortunately the lad had a very good head for heights. For example, he would climb up the trousers, crawl under the jacket, run across the waistband, hoist himself hand over hand up the braces, jump across to the tie, climb high inside its lining as if in a rock-chimney or crevasse, take a breather at the knot, then swing himself on to the lapel of the jacket and, from the buttonhole, slide down into the breast pocket.

49

This was only one of his astonishing mountaineering feats. I shan't describe all the others in detail. You know how it is: what I'm giving you is just a general idea. I shan't explain in any greater detail the why and the wherefore of Maxie's daily climbs. For the time being you must content yourselves with the fact that he himself knew what he was up to. But he talked about it to no one. And of course Winsome Waldemar also knew what Maxie was up to. But dolls and dummies know how to be silent as the grave.

Anyhow, the Professor was very satisfied with Maxie's progress. Sometimes he even called him 'Maxie the Mountaineer'. This was high praise which made The Little Man's eyes sparkle with pride.

Despite this rapid progress, the period of apprenticeship would have lasted another three months, perhaps even four months, if one evening the two tail-coats hadn't got mixed up. What two tail-coats? The Professor's tail-coat and the haute-école rider Gallopinski's tail-coat. It was a crazy business!

Brausewetter the ringmaster believes to this day that the whole thing was an accident. But nobody else in the Stilke Circus believed that: neither the fire-eaters, nor the imitation Chinese, nor the ice-cream sellers, nor the tight-rope walkers. And the Three Marzipan Sisters didn't believe it either. Rosa Marzipan, the prettiest girl of the three, insisted that it was an act of sheer spite. I suspect they were right. Jealousy obviously came into it. For Miss Rosa Marzipan turned all men's heads. Although that wasn't her intention at all.

As soon as the sisters, in their brief gauze skirts and flesh-tinted tights, tripped curtsying into the ring, the spectators would stamp and clap enthusiastically. It was impossible to imagine a more delicious spectacle. The girls looked nice enough to eat. No wonder they were called The Marzipans.

And then, when they had swung themselves on the tightly stretched trampoline and started leaping high, higher and then yet higher, and turned somersaults, hung horizontally in the air or did breakneck jumps, the enthusiasm knew no bounds. One felt the three young ladies must be as light as ostrich feathers. Whereas in fact the three of them together weighed three hundred-weight, which is, after all, twenty-four stones!

Rosa Marzipan, the most beautiful, weighed about eight stone three. That is not very heavy. For example, I myself weigh about ten stone ten, and that's only thirty-

eight pounds more. All the same, no one would take it into his head to compare me with an ostrich feather or to kneel before me and declare I was nice enough to eat. That sort of thing never happens to me. In this life, things never go as we want them to.

For those of you who do not know what a trampoline is, I should like to explain that it somewhat resembles a spring mattress. You too must certainly have often jumped about on your bed and been delighted by the bounciness of the mattress, the sudden weightlessness you felt and the great bounds you could make. A trampoline is longer and broader than a mattress, and as tightly stretched as the skin on a drum or a tambourine.

Anyone who has learnt to jump on it and bound higher and higher can shoot into the air like an arrow, stay up for five or six seconds, and in that time twist and tumble as if he weighed no more than a balloon. That's the sort of thing he can do. But only when he knows how to.

And of course he must also know how to fall right on the trampoline. For if he didn't fall on the trampoline, but to one side, then he'd break all his bones. Well, the Three Marzipan Sisters knew how to do all this. They had learnt it as children from their parents, who had also been trampolinists in their day.

*

But let's get back to the mixed-up tail-coats. It couldn't actually be proved, but obviously one of the musical clowns, Fernando, had done it. In the ring, he would blow on a mouth-organ as big as a plank, and then on another which was so tiny he swallowed it at every performance, and would go on playing it in his stomach. The spectators always thought that very funny. The clown himself, however, had long been a martyr to melancholia and bilious attacks. Because he was in love with Miss Rosa Marzipan and she wouldn't so much as look at him. For *she* was in love with Professor Hokus von Pokus.

This made the clown mad with rage. And so one day, a quarter of an hour before the performance, he changed the two tail-coats in the wardrobe! He hung the haute-école rider's tail-coat, with his top-hat, on the Professor's hook. And he hung the Professor's magic tail-coat and top-hat on the haute-école rider's hook. Then he sloped off on tiptoe.

*

Then when the Great Gallopinski pranced into the ring on his ebony steed Nero, drew abruptly on the reins and waved his top-hat in salutation, Alba the snow-white rabbit popped out of the lining, flopped on the sand and, bewildered, began hopping round in circles! This made the horse shy and rise up on his hind legs. The Great Gallopinski patted his neck, trying to calm him down. Whereupon one dove, Minna, flew out of Gallopinski's left sleeve and fluttered all over the place trying to find the little table with her cage on it so that she could slip in through the open door. But the table and the cage had still not been placed in the ring!

The stallion began to curvet and capriole, flinging out his hind legs. The band played the waltz from the operetta 'The Chocolate Soldier' and hoped the horse would now perform his celebrated dance steps. However, dancing was the last thing in his mind: he raced across the ring as if he were pursued by a swarm of bees. The rider could barely keep him reined.

This made the audience in the front rows jump to their feet. Many people screamed in alarm. One lady fainted. The other dove, Emma, fluttered out of Gallopinski's right sleeve. He drew even more tightly on the reins. Then the stallion leaped with all four hooves off the ground and gave a mad whinny. The horseman grabbed for his whip to hit the unmanageable steed. But it was not his whip, it was the magician's wand, which all of a sudden transformed itself into a gigantic bouquet of flowers! The horse angrily snatched the flowers out of his hand and tried to munch them. But they were made of coloured paper, and he spat them out disgustedly.

By now the audience was in stitches. The rabbit was sitting up and begging. The doves were fluttering perplexedly round Gallopinski's top-hat. The band was churning out the 'Pomp and Circumstance' march. The rider gave his stallion the spurs in order to make him pull himself together and march in time to the music. But the black steed was not used to having the spurs stuck into his flanks in public. He lashed out with his hind-legs and didn't stop shaking himself and kicking out in every direction until Gallopinski, one of the best haute-école riders in the world, flew out of the saddle in one mighty arc and landed in the sand!

Then the stallion, on thundering hooves, raced out of the ring and back to his stall. The horseman got up and limped groaning after him. The spectators were beside themselves, the whole two thousand of them. The Big Top shuddered with their gales of laughter. It was the first time they had seen a conjurer on horseback, especially one who was finally unseated!

*

The ringmaster Brausewetter was standing at the entrance to the ring, shouting despairingly: 'It's a catastrophe! It's a catastrophe!'

Gallopinski, who heard this as he hobbled past him,

said, gnashing his teeth: 'You call it a catastrophe? I call it a dirty trick! A filthy dirty trick! Who was it did such a thing to me? Let me get my hands on him! I'll feed the rotter to the lions. Ow!' He held his back and pulled an agonized face.

The Professor dashed into the ring, grabbed the rabbit by the lugs, enticed the two doves until they had settled on his outstretched hand, and ran with them back to the pits, out of breath and nearly out of his mind. 'I've been made to look an utter fool,' he complained. 'If the President of the Magic Circle hears about this, I'll be brought before the Magicians' Union. Because I've damaged the conjurer's professional image.'

'But through absolutely no fault of your own,' Brausewetter said soothingly.

'I demand compensation!' Gallopinski roared. 'In the first place, I was laughed at by two thousand spectators, and then I fell from my horse!'

'I should be going on in ten minutes,' the Professor cried. 'I wouldn't dream of it now. After the Great Gallopinski has made my tail-coat a laughing-stock? Never! And his old nag chewed up one of my most expensive bouquets!'

'He spat the rotten stuff out,' Gallopinski yelled, jumping with rage, then again crying 'Ow!'

'Please calm down, gentlemen!' Brausewetter begged. 'The show must go on. What's to be done now?'

'Under no circumstances will I appear, not if you beg me on your bended knees,' the Professor declared. 'I shall take my animals, go back to my hotel and drink a whole bottle of cognac!'

'Dear Hokus, don't do that!' The Little Man called from his breast pocket. 'I've a good idea. Hold me up to your ear a bit. It's very important!' And when Hokus held him up, Maxie began to murmur and whisper mysteriously.

The Professor listened in amazement, shook his head and said: 'No. You must train for at least another three months. It would be premature.'

But Maxie would not be silenced. 'You're in a temper,' he whispered, 'and that is something we cannot allow.'

'No, Maxie. Not today.'

'Yes. Today.'

'It's too soon!'

'Please, please! Say yes! I'm asking it for my birthday. If you grant me this, I'll ask for nothing else. Not even the doll's set of drawing-room furniture.'

'But your birthday isn't for another six months yet.'

'That doesn't matter, Hokus.'

At that moment the Professor felt a few very, very tiny tears on his big ear-lobe. Then he drew a deep breath and said: 'Herr Brausewetter, I've considered the matter. I shall drink the cognac later. I shall appear! Announce my entry through the microphone. Do it yourself.'

'With the greatest pleasure,' the ringmaster cried, greatly relieved. 'And what shall I tell the audience?'

'Tell my public that this evening, for the very first time, I shall perform with my conjurer's apprentice. And the act is called: "The Big Thief and The Little Man"!'

9

Ringmaster Brausewetter placates the
audience. 'The Big Thief and The Little
Man', a premature première. Fat Herr
Thynne and Dr Hornbostel are robbed
of everything. Brown and black shoe-
laces. Maxie waves to two thousand
people.

RINGMASTER BRAUSEWETTER kept his word. Barely
had the 'Whirlwinds', two famous roller-skaters, disappeared from the ring, to great applause, than Brausewetter drew on his white kid gloves and signalled to the leader
of the band. The orchestra played a fanfare.

The ringmaster strode with dignity to the microphone.
There was silence under the Big Top. 'Ladies and gentlemen,' Herr Brausewetter said, 'as you will have remarked
in your programme, the next act is Professor Hokus von
Pokus. He is, if I may be allowed to express myself so, the
Grand Master of all living conjurers. To praise him as he
deserves would take all night. And no circus director has
that much time.'

'That's a dirty shame!' a rowdy shouted from the back rows. But the audience hissed him down, and there was silence again. Only a horse whinnied, far away, in the stables. Probably it was Nero being unsaddled and scolded by Gallopinski.

'Due to a mysterious contretemps,' – Herr Brausewetter went on with his speech – 'Maestro Gallopinski seized a magician's wand instead of a whip. Whereupon he realized that conjuring and riding go together as little as ... as rollmops and chocolate sauce, or as Cologne Cathedral and a railway terminus.'

Some of the audience laughed.

'The outcome,' the ringmaster declared, 'is doubly distressing. For our Maestro Magician now absolutely refuses ever to wave his magic wand again. I went down on my knees to him. I even offered him my stamp collection. It was all in vain. He is adamant.'

The crowd grew restive. Some gave him the bird and booed. One man shouted: 'I want my money back!'

Herr Brausewetter raised his hands protestingly. 'Friends,' he said, 'the Professor will not perform his feats of magic, but – he *will* appear!'

The audience clapped.

'What he is about to show you today has never been done before in public. Even I myself, the guiding spirit of this concern, have not yet seen his performance. What is in store for you, for me, for all of us, is a World Première!'

The audience clapped even more.

'I only know the name of the act.' Herr Direktor Brausewetter threw his white-kid-gloved hands high in the air and shouted as loud as he could: 'The performance is entitled "The Big Thief and The Little Man"!'

Then he bowed elaborately and departed. The band

58

played another fanfare. Everyone was waiting expectantly. And there was utter stillness.

*

'Well, this is it,' the Professor said.

'It is indeed,' Maxie in his breast pocket whispered. 'Best of luck, Hokus!'

'I've got my fingers crossed,' the conjurer muttered and slowly entered the ring. When he reached the centre he bowed and said, smiling: 'Ladies and gentlemen, today there will be no conjuring tricks. Today we shall simply rob you. Watch your pockets! Nothing and no one is safe from me and my young assistant.'

'Where *is* this assistant of yours?' cried a fat man in the second row.

'He's here right now,' the Professor answered.

'But I can't see him,' the fat man called.

'Then please come a little closer,' Hokus kindly invited him.

The fat man, groaning, got up, came stumping into the ring, gave the Professor his hand and said: 'My name is Thynne.'

This made the audience laugh.

The fat man took a good look round. 'I still can't see him.'

The Professor went up close to the fat man, examined his eyes carefully, patted him on the shoulder and said: 'There's nothing wrong with your eyes, Herr Thynne. They're perfectly all right. Nevertheless, my assistant is here. I give you my word of honour.'

A gentleman in the front row cried: 'It's absolutely impossible! Bet you twenty marks that you're on your own!'

'Only twenty marks?'

59

'Fifty marks!'

'Very well,' Hokus said pleasantly. 'Would you too be so kind as to step out here? We have plenty of room. And don't forget to bring the money with you!' He took Herr Thynne's arm and waited smilingly for the gentleman in the front row who had wagered fifty marks. Herr Thynne was smiling too, although he had no idea why.

The gentleman strode up to them and introduced himself. 'Doktor Hornbostel,' he grunted abruptly. 'Got the money with me.' They all shook hands.

'Now, how about it?' the Professor asked. 'Where's my assistant?'

'Plain silly,' Dr Hornbostel declared. 'No such person. Not blind, am I? Want to double the stakes? Hundred marks?'

The Professor nodded. 'A hundred marks. Just as you wish.' He patted him on the chest. 'Your wallet's fat enough. I can feel it through your jacket.' Then he rubbed the material between his fingers, undid the middle button of Dr Hornbostel's jacket and said: 'Best quality worsted, not an ounce of synthetic fibre in it, no creases, first-class cut, expensive tailor.'

'Right,' the Doctor said proudly, turning round on his own axis.

'Wonderful!' Hokus said. 'One moment, please. You've a piece of white cotton hanging here.' He picked off the thread and carefully smoothed the jacket.

Fat Herr Thynne cleared his throat and said somewhat indignantly: 'That's all very fine, Professor. Best quality worsted, expensive tailor and all that. But when does the robbery actually start?'

'In two minutes we shall begin, Herr Thynne, sir. Not a second later. Kindly check the time by your wrist-watch.'

Fat Herr Thynne glanced at his wrist and his face dropped. 'It's gone!' he cried.

Hokus helped him to look for it. But the wrist-watch was not to be found in any of his pockets and it was not on his other wrist. Nor was it on the ground. 'This is very, very curious,' the conjurer drawled. '*We* two wanted to rob *you* two in two minutes' time, and here's your wrist-watch disappeared already!'

Then he looked the other gentleman straight in the eye. 'Doktor Hornbostel,' he said suspiciously, 'I wouldn't like to suspect you, that goes without saying, but – did *you* perhaps, inadvertently, take Herr Thynne's wrist-watch?'

'Poppycock!' Dr Hornbostel shouted angrily. 'Wouldn't steal a thing, either inadvertently or as a joke. A highly respected lawyer like me simply cannot indulge in that kind of behaviour.'

The spectators laughed heartily.

Hokus kept a straight face. 'May I just make sure?' he asked politely. 'It's a pure formality.'

'Don't mind!' growled Dr Hornbostel and raised his arms. He looked as if he were being held up by gangsters.

Hokus swiftly searched all his pockets. Suddenly he gave a start. Then he pulled out something and held it up: a wrist-watch!

'That's it!' cried fat Herr Thynne, snatched at it like a dog at a bone, strapped it on his wrist again and said, giving Hornbostel a sidelong look: 'Well, sir, really! That's going too far.'

'I swear it wasn't me,' the lawyer cried, offended. 'Got a watch of my own.' He stretched his wrist out of his sleeve, looked blank and exclaimed: 'It's gone!'

The audience laughed and applauded loudly.

'A gold watch! Eight jewels! Real Swiss make!'

Hokus wagged his finger smilingly at Herr Thynne and then went through all *his* pockets. Finally he fished a gold watch out of the right inside jacket pocket.

'That's it!' cried Hornbostel. 'That's mine! Give it back!'

Hokus helped him strap on his gold watch with its eight jewels and said, winking at the audience: 'These two fine gentlemen have really been a lot of fun for me.'

Then he turned to these two fine gentlemen.

'Don't start quarrelling with each other. Make it up! Shake hands and be friends! That's right. Thank you very much.' He glanced at his own wrist-watch. 'In one minute I shall set to work with my apprentice. We'll rifle your pockets till you're scared stiff. But later, perhaps, we shall give some of your valuables back to you. It's well known that ill-gotten gains never do one any good.'

'You and your non-existent conjurer's apprentice!' Dr Hornbostel cried. 'Your hundred marks are as good as in my pocket.'

'All in good time, Herr Doktor,' Hokus said. 'The robbery will begin in a minute. Please look at the time, both of you. It's seven minutes past nine. Check your watches!'

Hornbostel and fat Herr Thynne took a look at their wrist-watches and cried out simultaneously: 'Gone again! Both watches!' Indeed, both watches had vanished!

The audience roared its enthusiasm.

Then Hokus raised an arm to beg for silence. But at that very moment a little girl shouted: 'Hey, look, Mummy! The magic man's wearing three wrist-watches!'

Everyone stared at the Professor. He himself gazed as if in astonishment at his wrist. Three wrist-watches were flashing on his left wrist! The people laughed and yelled and clapped and stamped their feet with delight.

After the uproar had died down, Hokus politely returned the two watches and said: 'Well, now, ladies and gentlemen, I really wanted to ask a third member of the audience to join me out here. As a sort of observer. But observation wouldn't have done much good after all. Do you know why?'

'Because you'd still have gone on pinching like a thievish magpie!' hooted a lady, as thin as a rake.

'Wrong!' Hokus retorted. 'He wouldn't have been able to observe anything, because there's nothing left to steal. In fact, I've taken everything now.'

He patted his pockets and signed to two liveried attendants.

They fetched a table and set it in front of the Professor.

'Now,' he said to Dr Hornbostel and Herr Thynne. 'Let's play Father Christmas. Turn round so that you can't watch me. And I'll put the presents on the table. It'll be a real Christmas treat, I promise you. However, you won't be receiving new presents. Only a few practical things which have belonged to you a long time. I shall not give you just anything you ask for, only the things you ask to have back.'

'Pity!' fat Herr Thynne said. 'I could have done with a new typewriter.'

The Professor shook his head. 'I'm sorry,' he said. 'We can't start asking for that sort of thing. Otherwise Doktor Hornbostel would probably wish for a Bechstein grand or a Wurlitzer organ. No, just kindly turn round and shut your eyes tight!'

Neither of the men wanted to be thought a spoil-sport. They turned their backs to the table and squeezed their eyes tight shut. The Professor himself made sure that neither of them was trying to peep.

Then he went back to the table and began to turn out his pockets until they were empty. There seemed no end to it, and for minutes on end the audience sat breathless. Meanwhile the orchestra played an old, almost forgotten tune. It was called 'The Policeman's Two-step', and was therefore admirably suited to the occasion.

Now I'm sure you remember how, when he was in Berlin, Hokus had robbed Hinkeldey the hotel manager, and so perhaps you'll not be as amazed as the two thousand people in the circus were. They went 'Ah!' and 'Ooh!' and shouted: 'It's fantastic!' and 'This beats everything!' One person even cried: 'I'm going crazy!'

The simplest thing will be if I enumerate in a list the objects the Professor unloaded. Here goes. He brought out of his pockets:

    1 notebook, red leather
    1 diary, blue linen
    1 propelling pencil, silver
    1 ball-point pen, black
    1 fountain pen, black
    1 wallet, snakeskin
    1 cheque book, Bank of Commerce, blue
    1 purse, brown, Russia leather
    1 bunch of keys
    1 car key
    1 box of cough sweets
    1 tiepin, gold with pearl
    1 pair horn-rimmed glasses with case, buckskin, grey
    1 passport, German
    1 handkerchief, clean, white
    1 cigarette case, silver or nickel-plated
    1 packet of cigarettes, filter tips
    1 bill for coals, not yet paid

64

1 cigarette lighter, enamelled
1 box of matches, half full
1 pair of cufflinks, moonstones
1 wedding ring, dull gold
1 ring, platinum setting, lapis-lazuli
7 coins, total value 8 marks 10 pfennigs

The audience kept roaring its delight, and the two gentlemen with the tight-shut eyes shrank at every shout of triumph and every burst of laughter, as if they were receiving electric shocks. They patted and fingered all their pockets more and more desperately and in the end could hardly stand it any longer. For their pockets were as empty as the Gobi Desert.

Finally the Professor went up between them, laid his hands on their shoulders and said, like a kind uncle: 'Dear boys, here are your presents!'

Then they turned round, dashed to the table, fell upon their possessions and, amid laughter and applause from two thousand people, hastily stuffed the things back into their jackets and trousers.

Because the spectators seemed as if they would never stop laughing, Hokus at last raised his hands, and silence reigned. The band, too, stopped playing. 'I am glad you are laughing,' he said. 'But I hope it's not unkind laughter. Just remember that my tiny assistant and I could rob each one of you exactly as we have robbed these two nice gentlemen beside me.'

'Tiny assistant!' Dr Hornbostel said scornfully. 'Don't give me that again! And don't forget our wager!'

'We'll speak about that later,' the Professor replied. 'Anyhow, I thank you both for your active support.' He shook hands with them, slapped them on the shoulders and said: 'Goodbye, and all the best to you on the long high-road of the future.'

65

The pair turned to go. But Dr Hornbostel had hardly taken one step before he stumbled and gazed in astonishment at his feet. He had lost a shoe and bent down to pick it up. Hokus came to his help and asked concernedly: 'Have you hurt yourself?'

'No,' the Doctor growled and examined the shoe in his hand. 'But the lace is missing.' He bent down to the shoe that was still on his other foot. 'The other shoe-lace is missing too!'

'Does this sort of thing often happen to you?' Hokus asked sympathetically. 'Do you often go out without laces?'

The people began to giggle again.

'It's downright ridiculous,' Hornbostel snarled. 'I'm not daft, you know.'

'Fortunately I am able to help you out,' Hokus said. 'I always carry spare shoe-laces with me.' He fished a pair of shoe-laces out of his pocket. 'Please take these.'

'Unfortunately they won't do for me. I don't want brown, but black ones.'

'I've got black ones too,' Hokus said and dipped into another pocket. 'Here you are. What's wrong? Are they not black enough for you? I haven't any blacker than these.'

'You – you villain!' cried Dr Hornbostel. 'These are my own!'

'Better than none at all,' the Professor remarked. 'And what shall I do with the brown ones? Perhaps Herr Thynne can find some use for them?'

'Me?' that gentleman queried. 'What for? I am certainly wearing brown shoes, but . . .' He took a cautious squint over his stomach at his brown shoes, size 13, and gave a shout. 'Hello-hello!' he cried, smiling. 'My laces have disappeared too. Hand them over, now! Otherwise

I'll tumble over my plates of meat on the way home. Thanks a lot, Mister Crookfingers! Why don't you become a pickpocket? You'd be a millionaire within a month.'

'But I wouldn't be able to sleep in peace at night,' the Professor answered. 'Sleep is very important.'

'Well, I'm just the opposite,' the fat man declared amiably. '*I* could sleep in peace at last if only I had a million!'

Before he could continue this account of his shady ambitions, he was interrupted by the sharp-eyed little girl whom we have already met. 'Look, Mummy!' cried the irrepressible child. 'That other man's just lost his tie!'

Two thousand people gazed at Dr Hornbostel the lawyer, who clutched suddenly at the collar of his shirt. And indeed his beautiful silk foulard necktie had vanished! When the whole circus burst out laughing, Hornbostel became cross. 'A joke's a joke!' he said glumly. 'Kindly return my necktie at once!'

'It's in your breast pocket, Doktor Hornbostel, sir,'

Hokus replied. Then he shook hands with both the gentle-men and thanked them heartily for their cooperation.

'You're welcome,' fat Herr Thynne answered. 'But leave my hand alone, will you? Or you'll be snitching that too!' He stumped back to his seat, taking cautious steps, so as not to lose his shoes. Half-way there he suddenly stopped and said: 'What's happening to my pants?' He opened his jacket and shouted, horrified: 'My braces! Where are my braces?'

'Take it easy!' Hokus called. 'Could I inadvertently have . . .?' He felt in his pockets and gave a start. 'There does seem to be something here . . . One moment, Herr Thynne, sir. I simply can't imagine how I . . . On the other hand . . . with my absent-minded ways . . .' And there he was, dangling a pair of braces in the air. 'Why, here they are!'

The audience was in stitches. And when Dr Horn-bostel, tying on his silk tie, nervously opened his jacket and felt for his braces, the people laughed all the more. But he still had them; he sighed with relief and mopped his brow. He was sweating with anxiety. Then he picked up the shoes he had tripped over and hobbled back to his seat in the front row.

The band played a fanfare. The trumpeters were laughing so much, they blew wrong notes. Fat Herr Thynne was presented with his braces. And Professor Hokus von Pokus bowed elegantly. 'The Little Man and my Humble Self', he proclaimed, smiling, 'give our thanks to the public for its exemplary attentiveness.'

Then they all clapped and cried 'Bravo!' and 'Wonder-ful!' and 'Fabulous!'

But Dr Hornbostel had hardly sat down before he jumped up, gesticulating wildly, and shouted: 'What about our bet? You owe me one hundred marks!'

The Professor gave a signal to Herr Brausewetter who was standing, beaming, at the side of the ring. The ringmaster passed on the signal. Then there rose slowly out of its trap the circular cage that separated the audience from the ring only when wild-animal acts were being presented.

'Now I shall show you my conjurer's apprentice, The Little Man. Now you can convince yourselves that he really exists. The grille has been raised only to prevent you, in your enthusiasm, from trampling him and me to pieces.'

Then the Professor turned to Dr Hornbostel. 'There! You have lost your bet. You need not give me the hundred marks. I have already extracted them from your wallet. Please check your money!'

Dr Hornbostel counted his notes, whispered: 'That's right,' and sank back into his seat.

Hokus took Maxie out of his breast pocket, held him up and cried: 'Allow me to introduce you all to The Little Man. Here he is!'

The spectators jumped up and lumbered down the steps, shoving and squeezing each other and pressing their faces close to the grille. 'There he is!' they cried. 'I can't see him!' 'Yes, he's there!' 'Where? Where?' 'On the Professor's palm.' 'Ooh! Isn't he tiny! Like a matchstick!' 'You'd hardly credit it!'

Then The Little Man laughed and waved to them.

IO

The radio patrol car intervenes. The
Little Man is promoted conjurer's assistant. Two kinds of applause. Gallopinski needs a new whip. Rosa Marzipan
throw her arms round the Professor's
neck. Maxie sends his compliments.

IT was a tremendous triumph, and order was restored in
the circus only after a radio patrol car with a wailing siren
and a blue light on the roof had arrived on the scene. It
had collected the Professor, The Little Man, the two
doves and Alba the rabbit and taken them by a devious
route to their hotel. The cars that tried to follow them
were thus shaken off.

A little later, Hokus and Maxie were sitting in the Red
Room at their hotel. They ordered a black coffee with
cream and two spoons, took a deep breath, looked at one
another and smiled.

The head waiter hung a sign saying 'Please do not disturb!' on the doorknob before he gave the order for the
coffee. He too had already heard of the sensational
success.

*

'Well?' The Little Man modestly inquired. 'Were you satisfied with me?'

The Professor nodded. 'You did a very nice job. As you know I really wanted to wait another few months.'

'But we had to do something,' The Little Man cried. 'We simply couldn't have just shrugged off the disgrace with your tail-coat.'

'What a dirty trick!' the Professor growled, and banged his fist on the table. 'Gallopinski was out of his mind. And the poor horse!'

'And our poor rabbit!' Maxie said. 'I thought it would drop dead with fright any minute.'

'Did you have a tough time?' the Professor asked, smiling.

'The braces were the worst. The left-hand front metal clip simply wouldn't come open. I broke two finger-nails. It's much easier with Winsome Waldemar.'

'But then it went so much better with the shoe-laces,' the Professor said. 'That was first-class work. And the trick with the necktie came off too.'

'Easy as pie,' Maxie recalled. 'The knot was quite loose. I was inside in a jiffy.'

'Yes. Silk foulard is pliable. That was lucky for us. Luck's part of the business.'

The Little Man wrinkled his forehead. 'I must ask you something, and you mustn't try to get out of it.'

'All right. Shoot!'

'I would give anything to know.'

'Know what?'

'Whether you now consider that one day I might become a real artiste.'

'One day?' the Professor asked. 'You're one already. This evening you passed your apprentice's test.'

71

'Oh!' whispered Maxie. That was all. He couldn't say another thing.

'Now you're my conjurer's assistant. Full stop.'

'Are you sure the people didn't clap just because I am so little?'

'No, my boy. But of course that sort of thing plays its part. When Jumbo the elephant sits on a pedestal and raises his front legs, people clap. Why? Because he can do something and because he is so big. If he were just a big lump and hadn't learnt to do anything, people would just as soon stay at home on the sofa. D'you see?'

'More or less.'

'There are two kinds of applause,' the Professor proceeded with his lecture. 'Let's take another example. When the Three Marzipan Sisters leap five yards into the air from their trampoline, and turn somersaults, the audience applauds enthusiastically. Why? Because they can do something and because they look so pretty.'

'Especially Miss Rosa,' Maxie suggested cheekily.

'If they were ugly, the three girls would not appeal half so much to the audience, even if they were able to jump another two yards higher.'

'Are there two kinds of applause for the clowns as well?'

'Yes, there are. If they didn't have fat red noses and baggy pants and shoes like ducks' bills, their jokes wouldn't be half so comical. It's always like that.'

'Is it the same for you, too?' The Little Man asked inquisitively. 'You aren't as big as Jumbo or as little as me. You haven't a red nose and you're not as beautiful as the Marzipan Sisters. What two kinds of applause do *you* have?'

The Professor laughed. 'I don't know,' he said finally.

'But *I* know!' The Little Man cried triumphantly. 'In the first place, you're a terrific conjurer . . .'

'And in the second place?'

'Lift me up, and I'll whisper in your ear.'

The Professor lifted up The Little Man.

'In the second place,' Maxie whispered, 'in the second place you are the best person in the whole world.'

At first there was a little pause. Then the Professor cleared his throat, and said, awkwardly: 'Mmm . . . yes. Well after all, it has to be someone.'

Maxie laughed softly. But immediately afterwards he heaved a sigh. 'D'you know, sometimes I feel I should like to be the same size as normal people. At this very moment, for example.'

'Why just now, eh?'

'Because then I should have really long arms and could fling them round your neck.'

'My dear boy,' the Professor said.

And Maxie whispered back: 'My dear, dear Hokus.'

Then at last the head waiter brought the black coffee with two spoons. 'The coffee-maker sends her best compliments and the little spoon as a present for The Little Man. It was the smallest spoon she could lay her hands on in the kitchen.'

'And why is it a present for me?' Maxie asked, astonished.

The head waiter gave a deep bow. 'As a lasting memento of the day on which you became famous. The coffee-maker has scratched today's date on the spoon with a larding-pin.'

'With a larding-pin?' echoed The Little Man.

'That's right,' the head waiter replied. 'It's mostly used for larding roast hare and saddle of venison. The cook couldn't find anything sharper.'

'Many, many thanks,' Maxie said. 'So does the coffee-maker think I am famous now?'

'Not only the coffee-maker thinks that!' called a lady's voice. The exuberant tones belonged to Miss Rosa Marzipan. 'Here I am!' the Marzipan girl declared. 'The first reporters and photographers and radio producers are already lurking outside the front of the hotel. But the doorman is not letting them in.'

'Good for him!' the Professor grunted. 'And how did he come to let *you* in?'

'I know exactly how she did it,' cried The Little Man, rubbing his hands. 'She just looked at him and fluttered her eyelashes.'

'You've got it,' said Miss Rosa. 'He melted like chocolate ice-cream on a radiator. The cleaner had to come and mop up the remains.' Then she gave Maxie a little kiss, because he was so little, and an even smaller kiss to Hokus, because he was so big. 'And now, I'm feeling hungry,' she declared briskly.

'Hungry for a kiss from us?' the Professor inquired.

'No, for saddle of venison,' she replied. 'A well-larded saddle of venison with potato croquettes and cranberry sauce. And you must try some too.'

Whereupon the head waiter really got a move on.

*

After dinner she said: 'Well, that's life, my friends. I enjoyed my meal, you are famous, and Maestro Gallopinski needs a new riding-whip.'

'What for?' inquired Maxie, inquisitive as usual.

'Because his old one's smashed to pieces,' the young lady informed him. 'It came into close contact with the clown Fernando for a few minutes. That was too much for the poor whip. And for Fernando, too, as a matter of fact.'

'Because of the mixed-up tail-coats?'

Rosa nodded. 'That's right. Though the clown wanted to make a fool of a certain Herr Hokus, not the rider and his horse.'

'Hokus?' cried The Little Man in perplexity.

'Fernando is jealous. Because he thinks Hokus is in love with me.'

'Well, he's right there!' Maxie cried.

Then the conjurer went as red as a blood orange and looked as if he'd like to vanish on the spot, if he'd been able to. Or to change himself into a toothbrush. But only absolutely genuine magicians can do that sort of thing.

Miss Rosa looked at him with sparkling eyes. 'Is that true?' she asked and slowly stood up. 'Is that true?' she repeated, menacingly.

'It's true,' Hokus said gloomily and gazed at the toes of his shoes as if he were seeing them for the first time.

'I could box your ears for you!' she scolded him. 'Why didn't you tell me, you wretch? Why didn't you fall on your knees before me long ago, you rogue? Why didn't you implore me to give you my marzipan hand and heart, you coward?'

The Professor replied: 'I'll give you a good spanking if you speak to me like that!'

She threw her arms in the air and cried ecstatically: 'At last! The first words of love!' Then she flung her arms round his neck, making all the dishes rattle.

Maxie again rubbed his hands.

After five minutes, Rosa Marzipan whispered: 'I regret every day I didn't know about your love. We've lost a lot of time.'

'Don't worry yourself about that,' Hokus said. 'You're still young, you know.'

'That's so,' she admitted. 'And marzipan keeps fresh a long time.'

After another five minutes someone near by gave a discreet cough. It was the head waiter. 'Maxie sends you his compliments.'

'But where's he got to?' the pair cried with one voice. They went as white as the tablecloth with shock.

'He's upstairs in your room. I had to take him up in the lift. He's sitting in the flower-pot on the balcony and reports that he is highly satisfied.'

'It's frightful,' the Professor murmured when the head waiter had departed. 'We simply didn't notice a thing. I'm an unnatural father.'

'It's high time there was someone to look after both of you!' she declared. 'Is the situation still vacant? I know of someone who'd take it.'

'I hope it's no one who goes bouncing about on a trampoline,' he said.

She smiled. 'I have no intention of spending the rest of my life turning somersaults in the air. I'm applying for the position, Herr Professor.'

'You're engaged,' was his answer.

I I

Maxie in the pot of lilies of the valley.
Frau Holzer gives a few sneezes. At the
Discontentment Doctor's. The Little
Man grows and becomes a giant. He
looks at himself in the mirror. The
second magic potion. A completely normal boy.

MEANWHILE The Little Man was sitting on the balcony,
in a flower-pot. It was a white earthenware pot. That
morning the hotel gardener had planted twenty lilies of
the valley in it, because he knew that they were Maxie's
favourite flowers.

'Is there a poem about the scent of lilies of the valley?'
the boy had inquired once. But neither Hokus nor the
gardener knew of one.

'Probably it would be as difficult as the quadruple
somersault,' Hokus had conjectured.

'But there's no such thing as a quadruple somersault,'
The Little Man had cried.

'I know,' Hokus had replied. 'That's the whole
point.'

*

Now, as we have said, The Little Man was sitting in the flower-pot, leaning against one of the tender green stems, gazing at the clusters of lily-of-the-valley blossoms above, sniffing the fragrance that even poets cannot describe, and thinking about life. People do that sometimes. Even healthy boys. Even The Little Man.

He thought of his parents and of the Eiffel Tower, of Hokus and Miss Marzipan, of the mixed-up tail-coats and Fernando the Clown, of Gallopinski's broken whip and Herr Thynne's braces, of the raucous circus and the gentle lilies of the valley and . . . and . . . and . . . And then he fell asleep and started dreaming.

*

In his dream, he was running, small as he was, down an endlessly long shopping street, feeling he would never be able to escape from all the boots and shoes. He was in mortal danger. The passers-by were in a hurry; they did not see him and went striding past and over him, taking big steps, so that he had to keep jumping, terrified by their soles and heels, in wild zigzags over the pavement. Sometimes he pressed himself against the wall of a house in order to recover his breath a little. Then he would run on. His heart was in his mouth.

If someone had stamped on him, no one would have noticed it. And Hokus would have searched in vain for his Maxie. Perhaps a street-sweeper might have come and swept him on to his shovel with the newspapers and cigarette ends and thrown him into the dustcart. What a deplorable and premature end for a young and promising artiste!

Look out! Another pair of heavy boots came clumping along. At the last minute The Little Man managed to jump clear! But in doing so he almost found himself underneath the sharp heel of a lady's shoe. In desperation he leaped into the air and grabbed the hem of a coat. He clambered up the coat until he had reached the shoulder, and settled himself on a wide collar.

The collar belonged to a duffle coat. And the duffle coat belonged to a woman. She did not notice that she was no longer alone, and so Maxie was able to observe her undisturbed. She was an elderly lady. Her face looked good natured. She was carrying a string bag and seemed to have bought all kinds of things. Often she would stop in front of a shop window to look at the displays. Once she sneezed and said aloud to herself: 'Bless you, Frau Holzer!' Maxie very nearly burst out laughing at that.

While she was standing in front of a linen shop, pricing the dish-towels, hand-towels, handkerchiefs, dusters and napkins, The Little Man got bored, so he read the name-plates on the house door next to the linen shop window. There was an establishment where children's dirty hands could be washed, a convalescent home for limp ginger-bread biscuits, and also a doctor's nameplate which the boy stared at breathlessly. Could he believe his eyes? The nameplate read:

PROFESSOR WACHSMUTH
Doctor of Medicine
Specialist in chronic discontent
Free treatment for giants and dwarfs
Hours of consultation: any time you like
First floor on the left

Just then, the lady sneezed once again. 'It's going to be fine weather,' she said to herself. 'The weathers are sneezing!' And yet again she fetched a deep breath and again went 'Achoo!'

Then The Little Man said: 'Bless you, Frau Holzer!'

79

'Thank you kindly,' she amiably replied. Then she started, turned in every direction and asked: 'Who was it who said "Bless you"?'

'Me!' Maxie cheerfully cried. 'But you can't see me, because I'm only two inches tall and I'm sitting on your coat collar.'

'Mind you don't fall down, then!' she said in a worried tone and went close to the shop window to examine her reflection. 'I think I can see you now. My dear young man, how tiny you are! A body doesn't see the likes of you every day. Won't you come home with me? Are you hungry? Are you tired? Have you a tummy ache? Would you like me to put you to bed with a hot-water bottle?'

'No thank you,' Maxie replied. 'It's awfully nice of you to worry but there's nothing wrong with me. However, I should be grateful if you would go next door and carry me up to the first floor and ring Dr Wachsmuth's bell for me. Bell-pushes are too high for me to reach.'

'If that's all you want,' Frau Holzer said stoutly. She marched into the entrance hall, stumped upstairs and on the first floor pressed the bell on the left-hand door. She stood reading the sign. 'Whatever next?' she said. 'A specialist in chronic discontent?' She laughed. 'He wouldn't make much of a living out of *me*! As far as I'm concerned, the doctor . . .'

But before she could say just *what* the doctor might do as far as she was concerned, the door opened, and she caught sight of an old gentleman in a doctor's white coat and with an uncommonly rich growth of facial hair.

He looked Frau Holzer quickly up and down from top to toe and shook his head. 'I think you've come to the wrong door,' he said in a sinister tone. 'You look so contented, you make all my corns ache.'

She laughed in his face. 'My! What a sourpuss *you*

are!' she exclaimed. 'You should go and see a doctor! Doktor Wachsmuth for example.'

'It'd be useless,' he growled. 'I can help everybody but myself.'

'You doctors are all alike,' Frau Holzer said and was about to go on. But again she was overcome by a sneeze.

'Bless you, Frau Holzer!' The Little Man said.

At that, the doctor's eyes popped out of his head. 'Well, strike me pink!' he grunted. 'Here's a patient to my liking!' And in a trice he had seized Maxie and slammed the door in Frau Holzer's face.

*

'Why are you discontented?' the doctor asked when they were in his consulting-room.

'I want to be bigger,' was Maxie's reply.

'How big?'

'I don't know.'

'Always the same story,' the doctor growled. 'Everyone knows what he *doesn't* want. But nobody knows what he *does* want.' He took a number of brightly coloured medicine bottles out of the glass-fronted cupboard and grabbed a spoon. 'How about seven foot six?' he drily suggested. 'I can't make you any bigger than that, or you'll be bumping your head on the ceiling. Well? Out with it!'

'Seven foot six?' The Little Man gazed up anxiously at the chandelier. 'And what if . . . what if . . . I didn't like it afterwards?'

'Then I should give you an antidote, and you'd get smaller again.'

'All right then,' Maxie said in a trembling voice. 'Let's try seven foot six!'

The doctor hummed and hawed behind his luxuriant

beard, poured into the spoon a few drops from a green bottle and commanded: 'Mouth open wide!'

The Little Man opened his mouth wide and felt a burning liquid on his tongue.

'Get it down!'

The Little Man gulped the green syrup down. It flamed in his throat and ran like wildfire down to his stomach.

Bigbeard fixed his gleaming eyes upon the boy and muttered: 'It's taking immediate effect.' And he was right.

There was a sudden thundering in Maxie's ears. There was a straining in his arms and legs. His ribs hurt. His hair and scalp ached. His kneecaps creaked. He saw rainbow-bright circles spinning before his eyes, with hundreds of silver and golden globes and stars dancing among them. He could hardly recognize his own hands. They were growing and getting ever longer and broader. Could these be *his* hands?

Soon he vaguely realized that the glass-fronted cabinet was getting smaller, and the calendar on the wall sinking lower and lower. Then there was a slight tinkling sound, because he had bumped the tip of his nose on the chandelier. And finally there was a jerk, as in a lift that stops too suddenly.

The bright circles before his eyes were turning more slowly. The globes and stars stopped dancing. The thunder died away in his ears. His hair no longer ached. His limbs no longer hurt.

And the doctor's voice was saying, satisfied: 'Seven foot six.'

But where on earth was Dr Bigbeard with the sour old face? Maxie looked all round for him. The curtain rod was right in front of his nose. The chandelier, which was still clinking and swaying a little, hung level with Maxie's chest. On top of the cabinet the dust lay inches thick. And dust lay also on the white-painted picture-rail that bordered the yellow wallpaper eighteen inches below the ceiling. In the corner high above the door a black spider was scrambling round its web. Maxie drew back in horror. In doing so, he knocked his hand against a high bookcase, and from the top shelf a book fell to the ground.

Doctor Bigbeard laughed. It sounded like an old billy-goat bleating. Then he cried mockingly: 'Would you ever credit it? I change him into a giant and the giant's frightened by a spider!'

Maxie glared down furiously at the desk. The doctor was still cackling away. 'Why are you laughing at me like

that?' asked The Little Man, who had all of a sudden grown so big. 'After all, I have no previous experience of being a giant, for until just recently I was only two inches tall! Have *you* never shaken with fear?'

'No, never,' said Bigbeard. 'Fear is something I have no use for. If a lion were to leap at me, I should change him, in mid-air, into a chaffinch or a brimstone butterfly.'

'So you're not really a doctor?'

'No. But I'm not a conjurer like your Hokus either.'

'Then what *are* you?'

'I'm a real honest-to-goodness magician.'

'Phew!' gasped Maxie. He held on to the cupboard to control his trembling. And because the cupboard was unsteady, both the cupboard and Maxie shook.

'Sit on this chair and look at yourself in the mirror,' the magician commanded. 'You still don't know what you look like now.'

Maxie sat down, blinked at the mirror, stared, and cried, beside himself: 'For heaven's sake! Is that *me*? Is that supposed to be *me*?' Horrified, he clapped his hands over his eyes.

'I think you look very nice,' the magician remarked. 'But we don't seem to have really hit upon what you yourself fancied.'

Maxie shook his head as if demented and muttered despairingly: 'I think I'm hideous. Beside a freak like me, a giraffe is nothing!'

'Then what size would you prefer?' the magician asked. 'This time, think more carefully.'

'I knew it right from the start,' Maxie said contritely. 'But I let my curiosity run away with me, and now I could kick myself.'

'How big *do* you want to be?' Bigbeard asked forthrightly. 'Don't beat about the bush!'

84

'Oh,' sighed Maxie. 'Oh, Mister Magician – I'd like to be the same size as any normal boy of my age. No bigger, no smaller, no fatter, no thinner, and no freak like a rare stamp or a camel with three humps and no cheekier and no more timid and no more clever and . . .'

'That's enough of that,' growled the magician and grabbed a red bottle and the spoon. 'So you want to be just an ordinary kid? Nothing easier. Open your mouth!'

Maxie the seven-foot-six giant valiantly opened his mouth wide and swallowed the thick red syrup. He even licked the spoon. His head ached. His ribs and joints creaked and cracked. His heart pounded. The bright circles whirled before his eyes like Catherine-wheels.

And then there was silence.

'Look in the mirror!' the magician commanded.

Maxie hardly dared. He raised his eyelids only a fraction of an inch. But then he opened his eyes wide, jumped up from the chair and threw up his arms, crying jubilantly, with all his might: 'Yes! Yes! Yes! Yes!'

In the mirror too a boy had thrown up his arms. A nice-looking boy of twelve or thirteen. Maxie ran to the mirror and beat with both hands against the glass, as if he wanted to embrace his reflection. 'Is that me?' Maxie cried.

'That's you!' the magician croaked, and laughed. 'That's Maxie Pichelsteiner, a completely normal boy of close on thirteen.'

'Oh, I'm so happy!' Maxie said softly.

'I hope you'll stay that way,' the doctor said. 'And now see to it that your progress continues.'

'How can I thank you?'

The magician stood up and pointed to the door. 'Go your way, and do not thank me.'

12

'What a silly peacock!' Extraordinary
posters in the town. Ringmaster Brausewetter is suddenly called Brausepulver.
Gallopinski is called Traberewski. They
have a good laugh at him. Not even
Hokus recognizes him. Max and Maxie.
It was all a dream.

Now at last he was just the same size as any ordinary boy.
Other children take such things for granted. But for him it
was something completely new. He was so proud of himself that he wished he could have stopped every passer-by
in the street and asked: 'What d'you think of me now?
Isn't it marvellous?'

Needless to say, he didn't do any such thing. The good
townsfolk would simply have been very surprised and at
the most might have answered: '*What's* so marvellous?
Boys of your size are two a penny.' They might even have
got angry.

Many gazed at him in wonder, even though he did not
speak to them. For he was radiant, as if he'd just won the
Pools. Besides, he behaved in an extraordinary manner.
Every so often he would twitch or even jump to one side,

as if he were afraid of being trampled on. At such moments he must just have forgotten that he was no longer The Little Man. And yet now he was seeing faces and hats and caps and not, as formerly, shoes and heels. But that's the way it is with old habits. They're more difficult to shake off than the common cold.

There was something even stranger: he kept coming to a halt in front of shop windows. And *not* to look at the pretty, interesting displays. But because of the – as *he* thought – pretty, interesting boy reflected in the plate glass. He could hardly get his fill of gazing at himself.

On one of these occasions somebody behind him suddenly said: 'What a silly peacock!'

This somebody was a boy of his own size, with straw-blond hair and a considerable gap between his two front teeth. 'This is the tenth shop window you've stopped to preen yourself in,' the boy accused him. 'I've never seen anything so sissy in all my life. Next thing you'll be giving yourself a kiss! Or proposing marriage to yourself!'

Maxie certainly felt a bit put out by this. But of course the fellow couldn't know the circumstances. So Maxie replied calmly: 'Leave me in peace!'

However, the straw-blond boy had no such notions of calm and peace, but went on taunting Maxie: 'You take steps just like a baby learning to walk. Come on, give me your little handie, in case you start falling on your face.'

Maxie began to simmer with rage. 'I'll give you my little handie all right!' he cried. 'Right on your cheeky little turned-up nose!'

'Oo, I'm ever so frightened!' the other mimsied. Then he began to laugh loudly at Maxie. 'He walks like a tiny tot and thinks he can put me on my back. Ha-ha-ha!'

That was too much for Maxie. His anger boiled over like milk from a saucepan. He swung his fist back, punched, and the blond boy went sprawling on the pavement holding his lower jaw with his left hand. Maxie also was taken aback. 'I'm sorry,' he said. 'It's the first time I've ever knocked anyone down.' Then he strolled on.

*

Apart from the mirror-like shop windows, what began to interest him more and more every minute were the posters. Wherever he looked, he saw himself. Though the posters were not true to the normal-sized boy he had now become: they showed The Little Man, the conjurer's apprentice, the tiny assistant to the celebrated Professor Hokus von Pokus who were appearing together at Stilke's Circus and drawing such storms of applause from their audiences. Maxie Pichelsteiner was everywhere to be seen and the slogans seemed to be tumbling over each other in their eagerness to catch the eye. The advertisements made nonsense.

In one of them he was leaning against a matchbox exactly the same size as himself, and the matchbox and Maxie were at least six feet high. The text of the advertisement ran:

THE LITTLE MAN
The newly-discovered Star of the Circus World
Sleeps only in matchboxes made by
SIRIUS MATCH LTD

On another poster he was holding in both hands a silvery, glittering, and much-larger-than-life-sized electric shaver, and the big letters brazenly announced:

The Little Man
Shaves only with
WISKAWAY
Super 66

Maxie thought: 'What cheek! When I'll have to wait at least another four years before I have the first hairs on my chin. Old Hokus'll be wondering what's up when he reads this rubbish.' And the rest of the posters were no better either. On one in which he was smoking a cigar, there stood, in big, bold letters:

THE LITTLE MAN
Prefers to smoke our health-giving
MANILA CIGARS
Highest Quality
. . . and what do *you* smoke?
From now on, only
MANILA CIGARS
Highest Quality

What queer people! The things they dreamed up to get rid of their stuff! Here they were trying to persuade the passers-by that The Little Man behaved like a grown-up. When everyone knew he was still only a boy. Up there on the left had been pasted yet another poster with his face on it. He was waving in his hand a glass from which bubbles were sparkling, and the text read:

THE LITTLE MAN
Like every other Man of Taste
Drinks on Festive Occasions
In the Company of Friends and Lovely Ladies
The International Brand of
Sparkling Champagne
FEMINA
Extra Dry

'What a lot of tripe!' thought Maxie. Hokus was quite right when he used to say: 'The advertising boys have a nerve!' Did the people who read this rubbish really rush into the shops and buy the shavers, cigars and bottles of champagne they were so urgently recommended to purchase?

The boy was about to stroll on. But then his eye was caught by a smaller and more modest poster, one he might easily have overlooked. There was no gaudy picture on it. And no photograph. But the words he read went through him like an electric shock:

STILKE'S CIRCUS
Come and see the First-rate Programme
Every Evening and Three Matinees
THE BIG THIEF AND THE LITTLE MAN
The Biggest Sensation of them all!!!
Laughter and Amazement such as
you've never known before!!!

Reserved seats at the box office

'Good heavens!' thought Maxie. 'Perhaps today's Wednesday or Saturday or Sunday? I must get to the afternoon performance. Hokus will be wondering where on earth I've got to.' And he took to his heels there and then.

Ringmaster Brausewetter was sitting in the centre of the ring, wearing his white gloves and black top-hat and reading a newspaper. He glanced up when Maxie came storming into the Big Top. 'Where's the fire?' he asked.

'Please excuse me,' the boy stammered breathlessly. 'But I don't know if it's Wednesday today.'

The ringmaster raised his eyebrows.

'Or Saturday,' the boy panted. 'Or Sunday.'

'Are you feeling quite all right?' the ringmaster asked

irritably. 'Here you come rushing into my circus and ask me if it's Wednesday! You might almost be charged with a breach of the peace.' Then he bent his head again over his newspaper.

'But Herr Brausewetter . . .' Maxie was thunderstruck. Why was the ringmaster so unfriendly towards him, the new darling of the public?

'You don't even know my right name!'

'Brausewetter!'

'From the day I was born I've been called Brausepulver,' the ringmaster declared vehemently. 'Not Brausewasser and not Brausewetter but Brausepulver! And not Juckpulver and not Schalfpulver but . . . well, what?'

'Brausepulver,' Maxie softly replied. He would have liked to sink through the ground. But then the haute-école rider Gallopinski came into the ring and asked: 'What are you getting so worked up about, Herr Brausepulver?'

'This young puppy's getting on my nerves,' the ringmaster growled. 'Comes running into the ring, asks me if it's Wednesday and calls me Brausewetter!'

'Clear out, you!' the rider hissed at Maxie. 'And double quick!'

'But Herr Gallopinski . . .' Maxie said, horrified.

'There you are!' the ringmaster cried, grabbing his black top-hat with his white-gloved hands.

'My name is Traberewski and not Gallopinski!' the rider yelled angrily.

'And today's Thursday, you blockhead!' the ringmaster smiled. 'Get yourself back home and do your homework.'

'Well, I'm an artiste,' Maxie shyly said.

'You don't say!' cried the ringmaster. 'We only needed that! What d'you do then? Eh? Give us some idea!'

'I can untie shoe-laces,' Maxie whispered.

Both men screamed at that, partly with amusement and partly with rage. Their faces went red as if they were going to have a fit. 'That's going too far!' the ringmaster roared.

And the rider shook his fists. 'So he can untie shoe-laces! We could do that from the age of three.'

The ringmaster was puffing and blowing like a walrus. 'I'm going out of my mind,' he groaned. 'He can untie shoe-laces! The boy's a genius!'

'And I can undo braces,' Maxie whispered, with tears in his voice.

'Now that's enough!' the ringmaster thundered. 'That's the height of insolence!'

'And I can untie neckties,' Maxie went on softly and tearfully.

At that the rider jumped on him, seized his collar and shook him backwards and forwards.

The ringmaster rose, moaning: 'Tan his backside for him!' he cried. 'And throw him out!'

'With the greatest pleasure,' the haute-école rider replied and laid the boy in a workmanlike way across his knees. 'Pity I haven't got my new whip with me,' he added. Then he set to work.

'Help!' screamed Maxie, and the word echoed round the big top. 'He-e-e-elp!'

At that moment Professor Hokus came into the tent from the stables and asked: 'Who's making that awful row?'

'It's me, dear Hokus!' the boy cried. 'Please, please help me! These two don't know who I am.' He tore himself free, ran to the Professor and repeated, beside himself: 'They don't know who I am!'

'Now calm down,' the Professor admonished him. Then he looked closely at the boy and asked: 'They don't know who you are?'

'No, Hokus!'

'Who *are* you, then?' the Professor cautiously inquired. 'I don't know who you are either.'

The boy felt as if an abyss were yawning at his feet. He felt dizzy. Everything started turning in circles. 'Hokus doesn't know who I am,' he whispered. 'Not even Hokus knows who I am.' Tears flowed down his cheeks.

It had grown very quiet. Even the ringmaster and Traberewski kept their mouths shut.

'But how should we know each other?' the Professor asked, at a loss.

'Because *I'm* your Maxie!' sobbed the boy. He despairingly covered his face with his hands. 'I'm Maxie Pichelsteiner! I am!'

'No! You're lying!' called a shrill boy's voice at that moment. '*I* am Maxie Pichelsteiner!'

The big boy dropped his hands and gaped, flabbergasted, at the Professor's breast pocket. The Little Man was peeping out of the pocket and waving his arms wildly. 'Take me away from him, please! I do not like liars.'

'Dear Hokus!' the big boy cried. 'Stay here! Stay with me! You're the only one I have in the world.'

*

'But Maxie,' the Professor was saying. 'Why are you weeping so dreadfully? Here I am beside you, and I shall always remain beside you. Did you have a bad dream?'

Maxie opened his eyes. Tears were still trickling between his eyelids. But he could see Hokus's concerned face bent above him. He smelt the scent of lily of the valley and realized that he was sitting in the flower-pot. On the balcony of his hotel room. He had only been dreaming, and all was well again.

13

It was a dream. A conversation before sleep. On the inventor of the zip-fastener. What is 'much'? Maxie is still not in the least bit tired. Mad lads and fast friends.

'Was it really only a dream?' The Little Man sighed with relief. A millstone fell from his neck. 'Oh, dear Hokus, what a good thing it is you can recognize me again!'

'D'you mean I didn't know who you were? Now listen!'

'Because I was too big,' Maxie declared. 'As big as other boys of my age. And yet at the same time I was tucked into your breast pocket, the size I am now and always have been!'

'Maxie and Max at one and the same time? Good heavens above! Then perhaps there's also a James and a Jamesie?'

The Little Man couldn't help laughing. His throat did still hurt a little. But he would soon be merry and bright again, he felt. 'Take me in your hand, please,' he said. 'There I can feel better how well you protect me.'

'In any case it's getting too cold out on the balcony,' Hokus said, and lifted him out of the flower-pot. 'You're now going to take a bath in the soap-dish. Then you'll lie down in the matchbox. And you can tell me, before you go to sleep, what you dreamed about.'

'Everything? The whole lot?'

'Certainly. The long and short of it, and the short and the long of it. Dreams are deep things.' Suddenly Hokus gave a start. 'Are you hungry? Or did you eat tripe and onions in your dream?'

'No,' Maxie said. 'It was a meatless dream. But all the same I feel I've had enough.'

*

With the bedside lamp lit, Maxie related his dream. The long and the short of it and the short and the long of it. About that nice Frau Holzer and her sneezes. About Professor Wachsmuth, who was a genuine magician and had changed him first into a giant and then into an ordinary schoolboy. He also told about his annoyance with the straw-blond boy. And about the advertisement kiosks and all their stupid posters. Then about the circus with ringmaster Brausepulver and haute-école equestrian Traberewski. And finally about the ghastly shock he had had when Hokus had come along with The Little Man sticking out of his breast pocket and had not recognized him, his own little Maxie.

Hokus was silent for a while. Then he cleared his throat and said: 'There we have it. The dream has given it away. You'd rather be a normal boy instead of The Little Man you are.'

Maxie nodded in confusion. 'Yes. That's what I've always wanted. Only I never told anyone. Not even you. Although I tell you everything else.'

'And when you were grown up you suddenly became anxious and afraid.'

'That's just how it was,' Maxie said in a faint voice. 'You once said that one must *be* something and *do* something. Well, I *was* nothing and could *do* nothing. When I told the ringmaster and Traberewski that I could undo shoe-laces, they nearly died of laughing.'

'Because you were big! Anyone can undo shoe-laces. Everyone's seen that. It's only when The Little Man does it, then it becomes something they've never seen before. Only you and no one else can do *that*.'

'It's not much,' said Maxie.

'No,' Hokus agreed. 'It's not much. That's so. But it's much better than nothing. For who on earth can do "much"? This actually happened: a man worked for years in prison to make a zip-fastener. Today you find it on suitcases and on many articles of clothing. That man invented the zip-fastener. Is that – "much"?'

Maxie listened attentively.

'Or someone runs the hundred yards one-tenth of a second faster than any other sprinter on earth,' Hokus went on, 'and people are so excited they throw their hats into the stadium. Well, I keep my hat on my head. A new record was set up? All well and good. I'm pleased too and clap my hands. But is that – "much"?'

'Perhaps it's *not* much,' The Little Man said. 'But what's *more*? And above all, what *is* "much"?'

'Preventing war,' Hokus replied. 'Conquering famine. Curing a disease that was considered to be incurable.'

'Neither of us can do that sort of thing,' Maxie said.

Hokus nodded. 'Neither of us can do that sort of thing. Pity! Our tricks don't carry us very far. We can only do two things. We can astonish people and make them laugh. There's no cause for us to get delusions of grandeur.

Nevertheless, tomorrow morning the papers will be falling over themselves in their enthusiasm over our act.'

'You really think so?'

'It'll be a sensation, my boy. There! And now we must sleep. Tomorrow is another day.' Hokus laid his head on the pillow.

'I don't really feel tired at all,' The Little Man declared.

'Herr Pichelsteiner, sir,' the Professor said. 'Would you be very kind, and have the goodness to blow out the candle?'

Maxie tittered and switched the light off. 'So now I'm little again,' he murmured in the darkness. 'Yet when you're near me, I feel all right.'

'You must sleep!'

'Actually, we're both pretty mad,' Maxie said. 'Don't you think so?'

'Yes, yes,' Hokus grunted. 'Mad lads and fast friends. And now you must go to sleep.'

'How do you mean, "fast friends"?' The Little Man asked. 'You don't look fast when you have your magic tail-coat on.'

'You must go to sleep!' the Professor growled, and yawned so loudly, even the lilies of the valley on the balcony heard him.

'And how are things with you and the Marzipan girl?' Maxie asked softly.

'You must sl . . .'

'I'm already asleep,' The Little Man said hastily and shut his eyes and his mouth. Whether he really did fall asleep at once I don't know. Firstly because it was pitch-dark in the room. And secondly, I wasn't in the room myself.

14

Fame in the morning. Telephone calls.
The first visitor is Herr Brausewetter.
Money isn't the main thing, but the most
important secondary consideration. The
rabbit in the wrong top-hat. Headlines
and rumours.

THE next day was a memorable one. Maxie woke up and
found himself famous.

The head porter of the hotel, who in his forty-year
career had acquired not only flat feet but also considerable experience, could be heard saying to the telephone operators as early as nine o'clock that morning:
'This is no flash-in-the-pan celebrity, girls. This little chap's
going to be as famous as the Leaning Tower of Pisa. You
mark my words!'

'We always do!' Fräulein Arabella guilelessly replied,
and the other young ladies giggled and held their hands
over the telephone mouthpieces.

But that day they didn't have much time for laughing.
Calls never stopped coming into the switchboard. The
whole world wanted to speak to The Little Man. Among

the callers was an excited female. She wished to know whether The Little Man were already married.

'I saw him yesterday evening at the circus,' the lady said, 'and I'm absolutely fascinated by him. Is he still available?'

'Unfortunately no,' Fräulein Arabella answered. 'Since the age of six he's been engaged to the Crown Princess of Australia. And she won't give him up.'

'What does he want to go down there for, among all those kangaroos?' the lady's voice said, taking on an irritable note. 'I have a shop selling babies' and children's clothes. It would be much more suitable for him. I beg of you, please connect me with his room!'

Fräulein Arabella shook her curly head. 'Completely out of the question, madame! He cannot be disturbed. Please apply for an appointment by letter. And kindly do not forget to enclose your esteemed photograph. The young gentleman has a great eye for beauty.'

Of course, not all the calls were as silly as this. But even reasonable telephone callers play havoc with the nerves and waste time when they come by the hundreds. The girls at the switchboard and the porter in his cubby-hole felt their heads spinning.

*

Meanwhile Hokus and Maxie were sitting on the balcony breakfasting in a quiet frame of mind.

'You shouldn't lick the marmalade spoon,' the Professor warned.

'Today it doesn't matter,' Maxie claimed. 'When one is as famous as I am, one may do such things.'

'You have a somewhat extraordinary concept of the nature of fame,' Hokus replied.

The two doves were perched on the flower-pot. The

rabbit was peeping out through the railings of the balcony. For the three animals this day so rich in glory was a day like any other.

The Little Man's eyes twinkled merrily. 'Minna, Emma and Alba,' he counted. 'All we need now is Rosa.'

Then there came three knocks at the door, and their first visitor appeared. It was not Rosa Marzipan, but the ringmaster, Herr Brausewetter. With one hand he swept off his top-hat, with the other he held out the morning

papers. 'A sensational success,' he bleated, and sank into a chair. 'The press, although not present at the performance, has outdone itself. Curious sightseers are swarming outside the hotel. It has put years on the liftboy. And the porter has lost his head and doesn't know where to find it.'

Maxie laughed, and Hokus glanced over the newspapers with the first short stop-press reports about his own and Maxie's enormous triumph. 'Things are moving,' he said in a satisfied voice.

'And moving upwards, Herr Professor,' Brausewetter added. 'Pity we have to part.' He gazed glumly at the floor.

'What-a-a-t?' The Little Man asked. 'I don't understand.'

Brausewetter wiped the top-hat with his glove. 'The Herr Professor must have got my meaning I think.'

'I have,' boomed Hokus, nodding.

'I've not had a wink of sleep this night,' Brausewetter said, and put the top-hat under his chair. 'I've counted and counted. It's no use. Stilke's Circus is by no means a flea-circus, but enjoys the gratifying respect of both the profession and the public. But since yesterday evening you two have become world stars, and that I simply cannot afford.'

Hokus replied: 'But you don't know what salary we're asking.'

'No. But I wasn't born yesterday. I know the sort of money you'll both be offered on all sides. I can't compete with that. Because I'm a reliable employer. Any other director perhaps would think like this: If I get that inter national number I'll be sold out every night, even if I have to turn the Bamboo Family out into the streets . . .'

'No!' cried Maxie.

'Or if I were to sell the elephants to a zoo . . .'

'No!' cried Maxie.

'Or if I were to give the fire-eaters and the Marzipan Sisters their notice . . .'

'No!' Maxie shrieked excitedly. 'That you must never do!'

'I don't intend to do it,' the ringmaster said stoutly, 'and that is the very reason why we must part.'

Hokus said: 'Put your cards on the table! How much can you pay us?'

'Four times what you're getting at present. But others will offer you ten times as much.'

'No,' Hokus replied. 'Twenty times. In fact, I too was doing a bit of reckoning during the night. And you, dear Herr Direktor, can pay us more than four times as much without pawning your top-hat or a couple of elephants.'

'How much?'

'Five times as much.'

Direktor Brausewetter gave a pained smile. 'But only if I give up smoking cigars.'

'Your tobacco dealer'll never believe you.' Hokus said.

'He'd be the last to,' admitted Brausewetter and gave a weary laugh.

'Have you understood everything, Maxie?' Hokus asked. 'But put the marmalade spoon down before you reply.'

Maxie laid the spoon down. Then he said: 'I have understood everything. We could earn elsewhere five times as much as with Herr Brausepulver I mean Brausewetter. And even then, only if he gives up smoking.'

'A smart kid,' the director remarked.

'However,' The Little Man went on, 'how would it be if Stilke's Circus, now we're so famous, raised its admission fees? Only a little bit. And if he were to pay that little extra to *us*?'

'A dangerous kid,' the director declared and began to sweat.

'Still, it's not a bad idea,' Hokus said. 'But let's get to the main thing, boy. You and I are now partners, and your opinion from now on carries the same weight as my own.'

'Great!' cried The Little Man and rubbed his hands with joy.

'What are we to do? Shall we stay with Herr Brausewetter? Or for five times his money shall we go to some other circus or to some celebrated Variety Hall like the Lido in Paris? Think it over carefully before you answer. A great deal of money hangs on our decision.'

Maxie wrinkled his brow. 'Do you already know what you would like to do?'

'I do.'

'I think I know too,' The Little Man declared. 'I should like us to stay with Herr Brausewetter. It was he who engaged my parents and he's always been good to me. Like an uncle.'

'Bravo,' said Hokus. 'So we're agreed.' He turned to the circus director. 'Our decision is unanimous. We'll stay on with you.'

'Oh,' murmured Brausewetter. 'I call that very noble of you.' Deeply moved, he passed a hand across his eyes.

'We'll discuss the details this afternoon,' Hokus said smiling. 'The business side of the matter, as you have noticed, is not the main thing for my partner and myself . . .'

'But?' Maxie asked inquisitively.

'. . . but the most important secondary consideration,' the senior partner went on.

The director bowed smartly. 'Naturally, Herr Professor! Naturally! Well now; may I announce to the press and the broadcasting stations that you are to remain with me?'

'You may indeed, old man,' Hokus said, nodding.

Brausewetter was already on his feet. 'Then I must get a move on!' He grabbed his top-hat from under his chair and in an excess of high spirits set it at a jaunty angle on his head. But the top-hat started waggling from side to side as if possessed. 'What's the matter with it?' he asked in bewilderment, and quickly took his top-hat off again.

Whereupon, with one big leap, the white rabbit jumped out! He was scared to death and hopped as fast as he could into the room and into his basket.

'Look here, you!' Hokus wagged his finger at Herr

Brausewetter. 'That's unfair competition! Alba isn't having anything to do with strange top-hats!'

The director laughed and wagged *his* finger. 'Tell that to your rabbit, not to me!' And already he was running as fast as his big paunch would let him, out of the room and out of the hotel in order to give editors, TV and radio stations and news agencies the piping-hot news of the great good fortune that had befallen Stilke's Circus.

Only a few hours later the readers of the city newspapers learnt the great news. The central city editions even printed it on the front page. The big headlines ran:

THE LITTLE MAN STAYS WITH STILKE'S
ARTISTES' LOYALTY DESPITE WORLD FAME
BRAUSEWETTER BEATS ALL COMPETITORS TO IT!
CONJURING PROFESSOR AND CONJURER'S APPRENTICE
RENEW CONTRACT

The story under the headlines, and on the radio too, was still quite short. For no reporter had happened to be at the circus the evening before. There were still no photographs in the newspapers. And the lady announcer on TV

106

also consoled her viewers with promises of appearances in the next evening show.

At first their success was not much more than a rumour. Who ever would have thought that the clown Fernando would switch the two tail-coats? And that Professor Hokus von Pokus would therefore decide to present The Little Man prematurely to the public?

All the same, two thousand spectators had shared the experience and seen the tiny conjurer's apprentice with their own eyes; so the rumours running through the town had four thousand legs. And because it was still only a rumour the whole thing was all the more exciting and thrilling and interesting.

That evening, before the second performance of The Little Man, over a hundred thousand people were swarming and pushing round the Big Top.

15

The second performance and the second
sensation: Maxie becomes a flier. The
Stilke Archives. A film offer from Hollywood. Exchange of letters with the village of Pichelstein. A royal gift from the
kingdom of Breganzona.

A HUNDRED thousand people! That was ninety-eight
thousand too many! They at once besieged the advance-
bookings box office, and after a few hours there was not a
single seat left for the entire duration of the visit, although
Stilke's Circus still had another forty days to play in the
city and the price of seats was raised by one mark.

Three delivery vans carried the money late at night to
the safe-deposit vaults of a bank. Better safe than
sorry, thought Herr Brausewetter.

The performance itself, the second performance that is,
was once again a triumph for 'The Big Thief and The
Little Man'. The people from the television studios had
come with their equipment. Photographers were perched

everywhere with their cameras and flash-bulbs. Reporters and home- and foreign-affairs correspondents sat with wide-open eyes and their notebooks on their knees.

For the other artistes, the evening, despite the sold-out house, was not one of unadulterated pleasure. For they all knew well enough that the impatient public and the press and guests of honour were waiting only for the appearance of Hokus and Maxie.

Yes, guests of honour were there also. The city mayor with a golden chain round his shoulders, his two deputy mayors, the city treasurer, the city councillors, the American Consul General, three bank directors, a host of film producers, managers and directors, and even the Vice-Chancellor of the university, who hadn't been in a circus for the last forty years.

Professor Hokus brought two of these guests of honour into the ring and at once, with the assistance of The Little Man, absolutely cleared them out: they were the city mayor and the American Consul General!

Maxie ended by swiping the mayor's gold chain of office and the Consul General's braces. The two thousand spectators were vastly amused by that. And when the American lost his trousers – who do you think laughed loudest and longest? The American himself! That made the audience more pleased than ever.

*

When the circular cage had been raised and Hokus had displayed his little collaborator to the astounded throng, he announced an additional sensation. 'Ladies and gentlemen!' he called. 'Now The Little Man will fly up into the Big Top on the back of his friend Emma the performing dove, and after a round trip high above our heads will return safe and sound to my outstretched hand!'

And so it was. The band stopped playing. Not simply because it had been ordered to. They couldn't have brought forth a sound in any case.

The only creatures who showed not the least sign of fear during the adventurous flight were Emma and Maxie. With his right hand Maxie held lightly the blue silk ribbon which Hokus had previously tied, with the greatest care, round the dove's neck.

Emma took off with the utmost smoothness, rose in a series of spirals right up into the Big Top, flew round the tent three times and finally glided lower and lower, in elegant loops, like a little white sail-plane, until she landed on the Professor's outstretched hand. His hand had never in all his life trembled so much. And the entire circus heaved a sigh of relief, like a giant awakening from a nightmare.

In the dressing-room Hokus said: 'I should never have allowed that flight. Never.'

'It was wonderful!' cried Maxie. 'And I am eternally grateful that you finally allowed me to make it.'

The two doves sat up on top of the dressing-room mirror, caressing each other with their beaks and cooing.

The Little Man rubbed his hands. 'Do you know what they're talking about? Emma was describing our round flight and now Minna is jealous. But she has no need to be.'

'Why not?'

'Because tomorrow it'll be Minna's turn,' said Maxie.

*

It would naturally be quite impossible in these pages to give a complete report of their international success. But the press officer attached to the circus collected and arranged with scrupulous care all photographs, newspaper reports, interviews and letters.

Anyone who is interested in such details must apply to the Stilke Archives. The press officer, an energetic and very pleasant man, is called Kunibert Kleinschmidt and is quite willing to give information to serious inquirers. (Enclose stamped addressed envelope!)

So I shall pass over these trifles. It goes without saying that in the illustrated magazines there appeared long series of articles with pictures, mostly very brightly coloured. The French weekly *Paris Match* used Maxie, standing on Hokus's palm, as a coloured cover picture. On television, millions of people could watch how Maxie secretly undid the city mayor's shoe-laces and drew them out of their eyelets. The American illustrated magazine *Life* offered The Little Man a hundred thousand dollars if he would write his memoirs and give them exclusive rights. An international doctors' delegation announced that it would visit Maxie to carry out, in the cause of science, extensive tests of the physical and mental capacities of The Little Man; then it would publish its report. The film company of Metro-Goldwyn-Mayer was negotiating for a contract to make a wide-screen movie starring Maxie and the Professor in the leading roles. A match company put in a bid for a licence to stick on all its boxes a label saying: 'Let The Little Man Give You A Light.'

Hokus accepted many of these offers. He declined many more quite flatly, or at any rate provisionally. 'But the film in Hollywood – surely we could make that,' Maxie suggested.

The Professor shook his head. 'There's time for that. Maybe later on. Take one thing at a time, nice and quiet.'

But I must give a somewhat more detailed account of certain things. For example, the business of the letter from the village of Pichelstein which arrived one day. It read as follows:

Dear Max Pichelsteiner, Sir!

Recently we were able to admire you on the television, which apparatus is the common property of the host of the Blue Goose Inn and thirty-eight other families besides. It was really great and we are right proud of you and of your artistry. We all knew your parents well before they left this village and you are their spit and image, a real chip off the old block. But even littler than they were, and almost more like them than they were themselves. We all yelled, he's a real Pichelsteiner, and drank to your health. It was all very splendid and unforgettable.

We were able to follow you from the shoe-laces right up into the roof of the Big Top, till we felt quite dizzy, and so we decided unanimously to elect you an honorary member of our Gymnastic Association, which you are as of now. We hope that this will afford you as much pleasure as it does us honour.

To our littlest man and greatest gymnast we send our heartiest congratulations as well as all the best to you and yours!

Ever sincerely,
FERDINAND PICHELSTEINER
(Chairman and Troupe Leader
of the Pichelstein Gymnastic
Association: founded 1872)

Maxie was so pleased with the rather awkwardly written letter that he said to Rosa Marzipan: 'D'you know what? I should like to answer this Ferdinand straight away. May I dictate the letter to you while I'm sitting on the typewriter?'

The Marzipan girl, who had recently started coming

often to the hotel room and helping Hokus with his correspondence, said: 'OK., young man,' put a sheet of paper in the machine, put the Little Man on the carriage of the portable typewriter and said, smiling: 'I'm all ears!'

Then Maxie dictated his letter of thanks to Ferdinand Pichelsteiner and, while Rosa was typing, travelled on the carriage to the left until the little warning bell rang. Then she would shove the carriage together with The Little Man to the right and the trip would begin again.

Just as he was dictating 'Your grateful Maxie Pichelsteiner, Artiste', Hokus entered the room. He had been down in the hotel lobby discussing business with the lawyer from a Nuremberg toy factory, and said: 'Office closed, ladies and gentlemen! Coffee and apple-pie on the way up!'

Rosa was about to release the paper when Maxie cried excitedly: 'Please, wait a bit! I've forgotten something important.' And then he started dictating another sentence which had nothing at all to do with his honorary membership of the Gymnastic Association:

Because all Pichelsteiners are very small, it may well be that in Pichelstein there is a girl of my own age and also of my own size. If this were the case, I should be overjoyed. Hokus, my best friend, would certainly have nothing

against it if she were to come and visit me soon and stay as long as possible with us.

'Naturally she would also have to bring her parents with her,' Hokus said. And Maxie dictated:

She would naturally have to bring her parents with her too. We would send the travelling expenses at once. And if you have no such tiny little girl in Pichelstein, but have a boy, then that would be almost as nice. Actually, I'd prefer a girl, because I'm a boy myself. What I often miss is a friend of my own size . . .

The Little Man held his head low while he dictated this phrase and travelled backwards and forwards on the carriage of the typewriter.

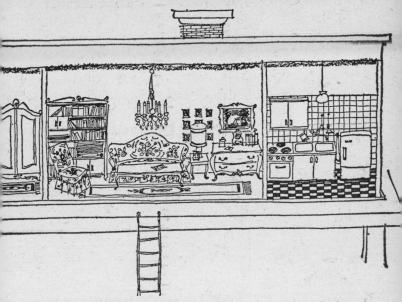

The Marzipan girl and Hokus exchanged a knowing look. 'I'll tell you what,' Rosa said to the little chap. 'You don't need to dictate the close of the letter to me with all the usual blah, I remain, sir, your devoted servant and all that. I can do that on my own initiative.'

Maxie nodded and murmured: 'Thank you.'

*

I must take this opportunity to mention yet another important letter. The sender was King Bileam of Breganzona. In his own kingdom, and also abroad, he had long been known as Bileam the Nice. And everyone who knows him declares that this is not nearly good enough. He should really be called Bileam the Nicest.

He wears a golden crown and a black hat, both at the

same time. The bejewelled crown is stitched firmly to the brim of the hat, and it doesn't look at all bad. But enough about hat styles.

Anyhow, this King Bileam also sent a letter. He, too, and his Queen and the Crown Prince and Princess had been enraptured by the TV programme. He hoped that Stilke's Circus would soon be having a holiday. Then The Little Man and his Professor absolutely must come at once to Breganzona to stay as royal guests in the King's palace. Princess Judith and Osram, the ten-year-old Crown Prince, could hardly bear to wait.

In the meantime, the two children had emptied their money-boxes and bought and dispatched a present for The Little Man, one which perhaps would give him pleasure.

*

Only two days later two sturdy packing-cases arrived. 'Royal Gift' was stamped on the cases, and that was no exaggeration. One case contained a complete, toy-sized residence: a living-room, a bedroom, a kitchen with an electric stove and a bathroom with cold and hot running water. Little lamps, water-tanks, changeable batteries – everything was there, nothing had been forgotten: it was a little miracle of construction!

In the second case there was a big, low table on which the four rooms could be comfortably accommodated, one next to the other. During their unpacking Rosa and Hokus had very nearly failed to notice and thrown away with the fine wood shavings a cellophane box. That would have been a pity. For in the box there was a narrow silken rope ladder which could be hooked on to the edge of the table and up whose rungs Maxie could clamber to reach his comfortable private dwelling.

This he did almost as soon as the residence had been set up on the table. He felt happy as he strolled through the rooms, switching on the lights and, on the cooking stove, in a wee pan, frying a morsel of beefsteak which the waiter had brought with a knob of butter and some chopped onion. They all had a taste, even the waiter, and found the sample excellent.

Maxie himself could not express any opinion. Because there was nothing left for him.

*

After the performance at the circus he bathed in his own bath-tub and told Hokus, who was looking on in amusement: 'Of course, this is something quite different from that silly soap-dish.'

Then he lay down in the heavenly soft bed in his own bedroom, stretched luxuriously and murmured: 'Of course, this is something quite different from that old matchbox.'

But the next morning, there he was lying in the old matchbox on the old bedside table.

'Well, now,' Hokus said. 'What's happened?'

The Little Man laughed in embarrassment. 'I changed round in the middle of the night.'

'But why?'

'The old matchbox is of course something quite different,' Maxie explained.

16

The Little Man at his own fireside.
Fame is a strain. And fame makes you
tired. The second letter from Pichelstein.
Nuremberg toy. A song becomes popu-
lar. Hokus makes the frightful discovery:
Maxie has vanished without a trace!

THE present from King Bileam and his two offspring pro-
vided once more, in that telling phrase, grist for the photo-
reporters' mill. They thronged into the hotel room with
their cameras, snapped the contents of the little dwelling
and bestowed upon the world new series of pictures with
terrific captions: 'The Little Man in apron and chef's cap
at his own stove', 'The Little Man taking a nap in the new
rocking-chair', 'The Little Man in front of the bookcase
with his miniature books', 'The Little Man in the heavenly
bed from Breganzona', 'The Little Man for the first time in
a bath-tub', 'The Little Man shows his rooms to the doves
Minna and Emma' – and so on, as if it would never end.

When all the hard-boiled newsmen with their cameras

and flashlights had finally gone, Maxie angrily tore his hair and shouted three times: 'Why aren't I The Invisible Right-Hand Man?'

'Fame is a strain,' Hokus remarked. 'That's the way it is. Anyhow, we'll stick the photos in an album and send them to Breganzona. The King and the King's children will certainly be pleased with them.'

'Let's do that,' said The Little Man. 'But we must decline the invitation for the time being. Fame is a strain.' Then he slipped into his track-suit and for an hour clambered all over Winsome Waldemar. After that he lay down in the matchbox, gave a mighty yawn and murmured before falling asleep: 'Fame makes you tired.'

*

A few days later there came a second letter from Pichelstein. Ferdinand Pichelsteiner, chairman of the Gymnastic Association, wrote to the honourable honorary member that the village could provide neither a girl nor a boy of Maxie's size. True, from time to time young married couples had set out into the wide, wide world. But, he went on, what had become of most of them was something which unfortunately . . .

. . . we have never heard. They haven't even let us know whether they're still alive or dead. Not to mention what's become of them in the world.

If we should hear of anything likely, we'll let you know at once. This I solemnly promise you: you can rely on the gymnast's oath. I am fifty years old and still active. Especially on the high parallel bars.

Your faithful namesake,

FERDINAND PICHELSTEINER

Hokus slowly folded the letter and said: 'Don't take it too hard, lad!'

'Oh, dear!' said Maxie. He was sitting in his tiny living-room on the green sofa and swinging his legs. 'Naturally it would have been lovely. All the more so now that I have a house. The girl could have slept in my bed. Because I like it much better in the matchbox.'

'But the new bed is much more comfortable.'

'I know, I know,' Maxie said. 'But it's too far away from your bed for my liking.'

*

Now have I already mentioned the lawyer with whom Hokus had spoken in the hotel lobby? He had come on business from a firm of Nuremberg toymakers. They had discussed and negotiated. They had come to an agreement and signed contracts. And then one day it finally happened: the Nuremberg factory sent a parcel containing ten matchboxes.

Ten matchboxes? Yes. Full of matches? No. But in each box there lay, in white cottonwool, A Little Man! Ten Little Men, as like our Maxie as peas in a pod! In ten suits of pyjamas, striped grey and blue, exactly like the sleeping-suit Maxie liked more than any other. The ten Maxies had moveable limbs. One could take them out of the matchboxes and stand them up. One could put them back again. One could lay them down, as if they were sleeping.

In short, it was a new toy that very soon afterwards was being sold in all countries and in all kinds of shops as well as at the circus, and brought in a lot of money for the toy

factory. Not only for the factory, but also for 'The Big Thief and The Little Man'. Their cut was eight per cent of all sales. That was why Hokus had bargained with the lawyer from Nuremberg in the hotel lobby. For Professor Hokus von Pokus was not only a celebrated conjurer, but also a very shrewd businessman.

You don't believe it? You think a shrewd businessman would not have stayed with Herr Brausewetter but – the devil calls the tune – gone off with a wealthier circus? Well, even a shrewd businessman sometimes has to act in a friendly way. Otherwise he is only an adding-machine on legs and one day will be completely fed up, not only with others, but also with himself.

I would not have said so much about the new toy if these confounded Nuremberg matchboxes did not have an important part to play in the next chapter. But please be patient a little longer. For . . .

For I should like, before we come to that, to tell you about a song that came out round about the same time and very quickly became popular. It could also be bought as a record. It was sung on the radio, and people danced to it in the dance-halls. The music was composed by Romano Korngiebel, conductor of the circus band. I do not know who was responsible for the lyric. The title was

THE SONG OF THE LITTLE MAN

I've even remembered a few verses. It began like this:

> What's all the fuss about?
> The folk they stand and blether.
> They ask each other whether
> They've seen The Little Man.
> They inquired of ten policemen
> Who really should have known,
> But all ten of them started to shout:
> 'Who? Who?'

After that, all kinds of people were asked if they had seen The Little Man. Until it got to this:

> A fat woman shouted then:
> 'I know him well and good!
> He sleeps till half-past seven
> In a matchbox made of wood.
> He breakfasts on hot chocolate,
> His weight is just two inches,
> His height's about two ounces,
> He often corresponds
> With nice King Bileam.
> The lad at even

Thieves in the circus like a raven.
Yet he returns it all
To the owners, big and small . . .'

Here my memory loses the thread again. I can only
remember the ending. Here we are told that anyone who
wanted to see The Little Man would have to jolly well
hurry up, because lately he had visibly begun to get
smaller:

After Tuesday you won't see him any more.
He's getting smaller day by day.
On Monday there's still a chance.
But on Tuesday, Tuesday,
Tuesday . . . He'll have vanished away.

'On Tuesday he'll have vanished away!' This last line
of the song was to become very significant. And indeed,
significant in such an awful way that I can hardly bring
myself to write it down.

Please don't be too alarmed! I can't change it, and I
must not conceal it. There's no help for it. But how on
earth shall I begin? Hold tight to your chair or the table-
top or your pillow! And don't tremble too much! You
must promise me. Otherwise I'd rather tell you nothing at
all. All right? Not trembling too much? Here goes:

On Tuesday he'd vanished away!
Who?
Maxie had vanished!
He had disappeared from the face of the earth.

*

When Hokus entered the hotel room, Emma and Minna
were hopping about distractedly on top of the wardrobe.
Hokus asked Maxie, who was lying peacefully in his

matchbox: 'What on earth's the matter with the doves? Have you any idea?'

As The Little Man did not answer, the Professor said: 'Hey, there, my young friend, have you lost your tongue?'

Silence again.

'Maxie Pichelsteiner!' Hokus shouted. 'I'm speaking to you! If you don't answer me at once I'll get the stomach-ache!'

Not a word. Not a titter. Nothing.

Then fear shot through Hokus as swift and sharp as a flash of lightning. He bent over the matchbox, then ran and flung open the room door, dashed out into the corridor and yelled: 'Maxie, where are you? Maxie!'

No reply. Dead stillness.

Hokus ran back into the room, snatched the telephone from its rest and had to sit down, so weak did he feel. 'Switchboard? Alert the police at once! Maxie has disappeared! The hotel manager is responsible for not letting anyone leave the hotel. No guest and no employee must leave! Don't ask questions! Do as I tell you!'

He slammed the receiver down, jumped up, went to the bedside table and hurled the matchbox together with Maxie with all his strength against the wall!

For it wasn't Maxie at all, but one of the confounded Nuremberg toy matchboxes with a little doll inside wearing grey-and-blue-striped pyjamas.

17

Excitement in the hotel. The false room
waiter. It smells of a hospital. Detective
Steinbiss comes on the scene. Maxie's
awakening. An important announcement on the radio. Otto and Bernhard.
The Little Man wants a taxi, and Otto
gets an attack of the giggles.

IT could only be a kidnapping case. But who had stolen
Maxie? And why had he done it? And done it in such a
carefully-planned way? For he had, after all, substituted a
doll for The Little Man, so that the abduction should not
be discovered immediately.

One of the room maids had seen a waiter coming out of
the room. No, she had never seen him before, but she
thought he must have been called to help out from
another floor. But neither the chief floor waiter nor the
restaurant had given such orders.

'So presumably he was not a waiter,' the hotel manager
said, 'but a crook who had put on a white jacket.'

The room maid asked: 'But then why didn't the little
lad cry for help? I'd have heard him, sure as sure.'

'They drugged him,' Hokus explained. 'Don't you smell anything?'

The other two raised their noses in the air and sniffed. The manager nodded: 'You're right, Herr Professor. It smells of a hospital. Chloroform?'

'Ether,' Hokus answered. He was in despair.

*

Detective Steinbiss, too, who was in charge of the investigation, was unable to offer any consolation. When he entered the room he was holding a waiter's white jacket. 'We found it in one of the dustbins standing in the yard. The man obviously escaped by the tradesmen's entrance before the hotel was closed off.'

'Anything else?' the manager asked. 'Any fingerprints?'

'Nothing,' replied Steinbiss. 'I've sent my men away. For the last hour they've been searching for matchboxes on everyone who wanted to leave the hotel. It was useless. There was no Little Man in any of the boxes. They all contained matches.'

'The airport, the railway stations, the main roads out of town?' Hokus queried.

'We're doing all we can,' Steinbiss answered. 'I haven't much hope. Easier to find the proverbial needle in a haystack.'

'The radio?'

'It is broadcasting our special announcement every half hour. Also the news of the reward of twenty thousand marks which you have offered is being regularly relayed.'

Hokus went out on the balcony and gazed up at the sky. He couldn't discover his Maxie there either. After a while he turned and said: 'I should like to increase the amount of the reward. Anyone who gives us final proof of where Maxie is will receive fifty thousand marks.'

'The radio stations will be informed of it immediately,' the detective said. 'Perhaps it'll be of some help. If we're dealing with a large gang, one of the kidnappers might well sing. Fifty thousand marks is not chicken-feed.'

'Why would he *sing*?' the room maid asked. 'Sing for fifty thousand marks? What use would that be to us?'

The detective made an impatient gesture. ' "Sing" is a professional term and means more or less to betray.'

'The whole thing's beyond me,' the manager said. 'For heaven's sake, what would anyone want to do with a kidnapped boy who's only two inches tall and as famous as Chaplin and Churchill? They can't sell him to another circus. They can't even exhibit him privately. Not for one minute! The police would be there in two shakes of a bee's knee.'

The room maid put on a conspiratorial expression. 'Perhaps they want to extort money from the Professor,' she whispered. 'Perhaps they'll only give Maxie back after he's placed a parcel containing a great big sum of money in a hollow tree under cover of darkness. That's what it'll be.'

The manager shrugged his shoulders. 'But then the gang would have to telephone or send an express letter.'

'Or maybe it's simply the work of a few maniacs. There's plenty of them about. If so, we're completely helpless.'

Who knows what else she might have come out with had not Rosa Marzipan suddenly dashed into the room, sobbing, and flung her arms round the Professor's neck, with the words: 'My poor Hokus!'

Behind her came, with measured tread, Herr Direktor Brausewetter. He was carrying his top-hat, and on his hands he wore, as always except when in bed, kid gloves. Today their colour was a medium grey. He put on black kid gloves only for funerals and white ones only for happy and festive occasions. He was most particular about the colour of his kid gloves.

'My dear Herr Professor,' he cried, 'we are all deeply distressed, and I wish to convey to you the sympathy of all your colleagues. At the general meeting of employees ten minutes ago we passed the unanimous resolution not to give any more performances until The Little Man is once more in our midst. Until then, Stilke's Circus will remain closed.'

'What's the use of that?' the room maid asked.

Brausewetter gave her a sharp look. 'It's primarily a gesture of friendship and solidarity, my dear.'

'And it may even be of some help,' Steinbiss declared. 'It will increase the alertness of the general public.'

Rosa Marzipan shook her locks. 'There's only one person who can help us in this.'

The manager opened his eyes wide. 'Who's that?'

'You're quite right,' Hokus told Rosa. 'He's our only hope.'

'But *who*?' repeated the manager.

Miss Marzipan said simply: 'Maxie himself!'

*

When The Little Man came to his senses, his head was throbbing. Yes, he was still lying in his matchbox. But he didn't recognize that light hanging from the ceiling. Where on earth was he?

Dance music was coming from a radio set. Blue cigarette-smoke was swimming on the air. And suddenly a surly man's voice said: 'Otto, see if the dwarf's wakened up at last.' Because nobody moved the voice went on angrily: 'Would you rather I sent you a written invitation?'

'You're too hasty, that's what's the matter with you,' another voice answered good-naturedly. 'It can't be good for your health, Bernard. Remember your heart!' But then a chair was scraped back. Someone stood up heavily and slowly came closer. Obviously it was the man called Otto.

Maxie shut his eyes, breathed regularly and felt someone bending over him. Otto was breathing hard, and he smelt like a cigarette factory standing next to a spirits factory. 'The little fellow's still asleep,' said Otto's voice. 'Let's hope you didn't give him too big a whiff of ether, Bernard old cock. Otherwise Señor Lopez will have one of his Negro gentlemen give your skull a nice going-over.'

'Shut your trap!' Bernard's voice growled. 'I carried out the deal as planned . . .'

At that moment the dance music broke off on the radio,

and a third voice announced: 'Attention! Stand by! We're going to repeat an important message!'

'If it's not from the cops, I'll eat my hat ...' Otto began.

'Quiet!' hissed Bernard.

Maxie held his breath and pricked up his ears.

'As we have already announced,' the radio announcer said, 'this morning The Little Man, well known to you all, was kidnapped from his hotel room. The kidnapper had disguised himself as a floor waiter. The white jacket used by him for this purpose has been identified. The Criminal Investigation Bureau is asking the public for their strongest support. Professor Hokus von Pokus has raised the reward he is offering to fifty thousand marks. Any relevant information should be passed on to this radio station or directly to Detective Inspector Steinbiss. Stilke's Circus has announced that all performances are cancelled until further notice. End of the message!' Then the dance music started again.

After a pause, Otto could be heard saying in awestruck tones: 'By gum! This Hokuspokus is really making a splash! Fifty thousand? I call that easy money! Don't you think so, Bernard? What about it?'

'You always were and always will be a thorough block-head,' Bernard's voice growled. 'Fifty thousand? You don't give up a permanent position for that kind of money.'

'All right,' Otto murmured. 'It was just an idea.'

'You're not the one who has ideas,' Bernard answered roughly. 'Leave that to me, got it? Right. Now I'm going to telephone.' A chair was pushed back violently. 'And keep a good watch on the dwarf while I'm out!'

*

When the room door had closed, Maxie ventured to open his eyes a fraction. There at an untidy table squatted a huge, bald-headed man, holding up an empty bottle to the light. So that was Otto!

'Drink's bad. No drink's even worse,' Otto muttered to himself and put down the bottle so hard that the table shook.

'Now or never!' thought Maxie and pretended to wake up. He gave such a jerk that the matchbox almost overturned. Then he shouted: 'Help! Where am I?' Then he gazed about him in bewilderment, whimpered and put both hands over his mouth. It was a virtuoso piece of acting.

Otto, taken completely by surprise, got an extra-ordinary shock. He leaped from his chair and hissed angrily: 'Will you shut your trap, you little monkey?'

Maxie yelled: 'I want to know where I am! How dare you talk to me like that! And who are you anyhow? Help! Hokus! He-e-e-lp!' He yelled so loud because he thought someone in the vicinity might hear him. But nothing stirred. No one had heard him. Apart from this besotted bald man called Otto.

'If you start bellowing again, I'll put a yard of sticking-plaster on your gob,' Otto said grimly.

'I don't care for your tone,' Maxie retorted. 'Kindly call me a taxi.'

Whereupon Otto was overcome with a fit of the giggles. It was, to be more precise, a mixture of laughter, coughing, sneezing and wheezing. It seemed highly prob-able that he might explode at any minute. But he did not explode. When he had finally gained control over himself again, he wiped the tears from his eyes and gasped: 'A taxi? If that's all you need, sir! Bernard's just gone out to inquire about a plane!'

18

Who bought the waiter's white jacket?
Great excitement at 'The Golden Ham'.
A report in the evening newspaper. Bald
Otto bellows. The empty house. Bernard
is the more dangerous. At night, Maxie
explores the horrible room.

THE white jacket had been bought in the city centre two
days before The Little Man was kidnapped. In a shop
that specialized in professional uniforms. This is what the
police finally established. At this shop one could buy
butchers' aprons, chefs' hats, doctors' smocks, nurses'
caps, canal-workers' overalls, divers' helmets, sleeve-
protectors for book-keepers, knee-pads for parquet-floor-
layers and mosaic-tilers – in short, it was a big, lively
emporium. And the assistants had been extremely ob-
liging to the gentlemen from the Criminal Investigation
Bureau. But nobody could now remember who had
bought the waiter's white jacket nor what he had looked
like.

*

Rosa Marzipan had persuaded Hokus to go out to a restaurant with her. 'You really must have something to eat,' she had declared. 'You can't go on sitting in your hotel room staring at the walls. That doesn't get us anywhere at all. And you'll fall ill yourself in the end.'

So now they were sitting in 'The Golden Ham', as the inn was called, and Hokus was staring, not at the wall, but at his plate. He couldn't swallow a bite nor could he utter a word. It had been like this for the past day and a half, and Miss Marzipan was becoming seriously worried. He had sipped a cup of consommé. That was all.

In order to console him, she said: 'Maxie will be back again tomorrow or the day after tomorrow at the latest. He's much too smart and clever to allow himself to be shut up for longer than that. Wild horses wouldn't stop him from escaping!'

'Unfortunately it's not horses that are stopping him,' Hokus retorted. 'It's crooks. Who knows what they have done to the little chap?' He sighed. Then he shook his head. 'Not even the higher reward seems to tempt them! And I was hoping that it would make them telephone to me straight away.'

'They're afraid of the police.'

'For Maxie's sake I would not have given them away,' Hokus murmured and stared down at his plate. Rosa Marzipan too had no appetite. However, she didn't show it too much, but ate a few bits because she thought he might absent-mindedly eat along with her. But it was love's labour lost.

While she was shoving her veal goulash around with her fork, a guest at one of the other tables suddenly jumped up and boxed resoundingly the ears of a newspaper seller who was going the rounds with the latest evening edition. 'What's got into you?' the gentleman yelled. 'Put my matchbox back on the table at once!'

'Bravo!' cried someone at the next table. 'I should have given him a good slap on the kisser too.'

'He tried the same thing on me,' cried a third. 'Waiter, bring the manager!'

There was quite an uproar. The newspaper seller was holding his cheek. The guests were holding the newspaper seller. The head waiter brought the manager. The manager signalled to a page-boy. The page-boy brought a policeman from the street corner. The policeman drew his notebook out of his pocket.

'I've no idea what's got into you all!' the newspaper seller complained. 'We hear all the time on the radio that the public should be on the look-out because The Little Man has been kidnapped. And then when one *is* on the look-out and sets an example by peeping into strangers' matchboxes to see if The Little Man is perhaps hidden inside, one gets boxed over the ear-hole. I don't like that sort of thing, constable!'

No sooner had the guests and the policeman heard this than they were all filled with remorse and contrition. They all apologized to one another. And even the newspaper seller was no longer angry. In a twinkling he sold all his evening papers from the sack hung round his neck, and departed satisfied. The policeman was invited to have a glass of beer on the house.

Everywhere one looked, there was someone studying the evening paper. Although it was the latest edition, there was nothing new in it about Maxie. Nevertheless the crime reporter had written a short article about the unsolved crime. All the guests at 'The Golden Ham' were reading it, and letting their food grow cold. Rosa Marzipan and Hokus too, leaning close together, were reading

135

the newspaper. At the top right-hand side of the front page there stood:

LITTLE MAN MYSTERY

Where is he? Where has he been hidden? On what street? In which house? Which room? An entire city is holding its breath. An entire city is helpless. Detective Inspector Steinbiss shrugs his shoulders. He and his men are looking haggard. What have they found so far? A waiter's white jacket in a dustbin. And the shop where the white jacket was purchased.

What else? Nothing. What did the purchaser look like? Was it 'the false waiter'? Or was it an accomplice? Did the criminal who kidnapped Our Little Man get into a waiting car? Did he lose himself among the crowds strolling on the pavements?

The criminal police are ceaselessly investigating hundreds of leads that have come in by telephone and by letter from all levels of the population. The work is colossal. The effort is staggering. The result – nothing. Nevertheless we should not relax our vigilance.

Even though a thousand clues lead to nothing, our trouble would be richly rewarded if the thousand-and-first clue helped to bring back to us, safe and sound, The Little Man, that darling of the public.

Yes, it was bad. Very bad. No one knew the street, the house or the room where Maxie was being held prisoner. And what a lot of streets, houses and rooms there are in a city with more than a million inhabitants!

Not even Maxie himself knew where he was. He only knew the room in which Bernard and bald, drunken Otto were guarding him. And that was one of those cheaply furnished rooms which resemble one another like ready-made suits. But even if it had been a room with Venetian mirrors and a self-portrait by Goya on the walls, what use would that have been to The Little Man? That wouldn't have told him the number of the house and the name of the street.

In one respect he had the lead over Hokus, Rosa Marzipan, the police, the circus and the rest of the world: he knew without a doubt that he was still alive and in good health! That was something the rest of the world did not know. And Maxie was very worried lest Hokus should be very worried about it. Yes, it was really bad. Very bad.

The two crooks were watching him like hawks. Usually the pair of them. They never left him alone for even half a second. At night it was the same thing. One would always be sitting beside his matchbox keeping guard over him. They took turns to go out and eat. And in order not to attract attention they ate every day in a different restaurant.

Otto fried and boiled Maxie's tiny meals on a propane gas stove. He made a pretty bad job of it, although he tried rather hard. 'Now eat it all up,' he would always say. 'Because if you fall sick or kick the bucket, Lopez'll have our lights and our livers.'

'But who *is* this Señor Lopez?' Maxie asked.

'Don't you go sticking your nose into other people's business!' Otto surlily replied and blinked at him angrily with his red-rimmed little eyes.

Maxie smiled and was silent. Then he said suddenly: 'Please open the window. I need some fresh air.'

Groaning, Otto stood up, opened the window and sat down again.

After a while Maxie pretended to be freezing. 'I'm freezing. Please close the window!'

Groaning, Otto stood up again, closed the window and sat down again.

Five minutes later Maxie asked: 'Is there still a bit of the pineapple tart left?'

Groaning, Otto stood up, looked into the cupboard, sat down again and grunted: 'No. You've gobbled it all up.'

'Please go to the cake-shop and bring me another one.'

'No!' bawled Otto, making the walls shake. 'No!' he bellowed, 'you little varmint!' Then he bethought himself that he was responsible for Maxie's well-being, pulled himself together and declared, as gently as he could: 'I'll bring you one when Bernard's come back from lunch.'

'Many thanks,' said Maxie in a friendly way and waited tensely for something to happen. For someone to knock on the door or ring the bell or for someone in the house to come angrily inquiring why there was all this frightful row at midday. For this was the only reason he was now provoking bald Otto to become white with rage. Let the fellow bellow! As if he were on a spit, roasting slowly!

'Remarkable,' The Little Man thought to himself. 'After all, there must be a whole house attached to these two rooms . . . And after all, in a house there are people living . . . but no one knocks and no one rings . . . Where *can* I be?' He did not show what he was feeling. But deep inside he was terribly afraid. Can you understand that? He acted cool as a cucumber. And yet he was shaking like a leaf.

He was most afraid of Bernard, because *he* never bellowed. His voice rang as chill as if it had just been brought out of the refrigerator. Whenever he spoke, one froze. And Maxie took care not to provoke him. Fortunately Bernard was frequently away from the house. When he came back, Otto would always ask: 'Anything new?' and

Bernard mostly answered 'No.' Or: 'If there's anything new I'll be telling you about it.' Or: 'Shut your trap!' Or: 'Go on! Go and eat! Get out!'

Only once did Otto blow his top with Bernard. He bellowed: 'I'm sick and tired of sticking around this dump and playing the nursemaid to a dwarf! When in creation are we going to hit the trail!'

Bernard looked the other up and down as if he were an old chained watchdog. Then he said: 'We are to wait until the cops are not so jumpy. Might be a couple of days or so.'

'What a drag!' Otto complained. 'If I had my way, we'd not be sitting here.'

Bernard nodded. 'That's so! If you had your way, we'd be sitting in clink.'

Otto slurped his glass of brandy empty, stood up groaning and shoved off grumbling to his lunch. Now Bernard lowered himself into the empty chair and read the newspaper with a bored look.

After a while Maxie asked, putting on a face as innocent as the flowers in May: 'Where are we going on our trip?'

'Sometimes I'm a bit hard of hearing,' Bernard answered, without lowering the newspaper.

'If that's all,' the boy said, 'I can speak louder!' And at once he yelled and screamed: 'Where are we going on our trip?'

At that, Bernard slowly put down the newspaper. 'I've got you now,' he said slowly. He was green with fury. 'But don't try anything on, you little half-dwarf. No one can hear you here.' He picked his paper up again. 'All the same, I advise you to watch your step. Because it's my job to deliver you alive. Alive and as well as possible. I'll get a tidy bit of cash for that. And so it's up to me to see you don't get sick or get stepped on with my heel? You get me?'

'More or less,' said Maxie, and endeavoured to stop his teeth from chattering.

'Any rate, if you try to pull anything on me, I'll cut my losses. Many a bigger dwarf than you has suddenly died.'

Maxie got goose-flesh all over.

'So you be a good kid,' Bernard went on, 'and think about your precious health.' Then he opened the newspaper again and began to read the sports news.

*

Maxie's worries and cares were getting bigger and bigger. The police and Hokus couldn't find him. The higher reward had led to nothing. And he himself no longer knew what to think.

At night, while bald Otto lay sleeping on the couch, he had naturally explored the room. He had clambered down the table-cloth and up the curtain to the window. What had he seen? On the other side of the street a row of houses. In the distance a church tower. And the window was bolted.

He had crawled around the floor and had thoroughly

140

examined the walls and, above all, the door-frames. But nowhere was there the slightest chink through which he might have squeezed himself. And what would have happened next, anyhow, if he had found himself standing in the corridor? There would be more doors. The door of the flat. The door of the house. Those two at least.

But it was pretty useless to think about chinks that did not exist. He was stuck in that confounded room as immovably as a nail in the wall. And time was passing and could not be halted. Soon the two villains, whose Christian names alone he knew, would be sitting in some aeroplane. With an unobtrusive matchbox in Bernard's jacket pocket.

And in the matchbox there would be no matches. Instead there would by lying there, nicely chloroformed for a few hours, a certain Maxie Pichelsteiner, the celebrated Little Man, who would never be seen or heard of again. The world would never hear of him again, and, what was worse, neither would the famous conjurer and circus professor Hokus von Pokus.

Maxie ground his teeth. 'I must get a move on,' he thought. 'I must get out of this room. As quickly as possible. No go? No ideas? Am I too stupid for that? That *would* be a joke!'

19

Detailed report on Señor Lopez. The
castle in South America. Pictures by
Remembring and Inkasso. Plane tickets
for Friday. Stomach-ache, not quite
genuine. Bald Otto runs to the chemist's.
Maxie sits on a garden gate.

WEDNESDAY was an eventful day. By mid-morning
Otto was already quite tipsy and started throwing out bits
of free information about the mysterious Señor Lopez.
Later Bernard came back from town and showed Otto the
flight tickets for Friday which he had just bought, but
went out again immediately, because he was hungry.

'I'll be eating at "The Loaded Dice",' he said, 'and I'll
come and relieve you in an hour.'

'All right,' said Otto. 'If you have pickled pork and
sauerkraut you can bring me up two portions. That'll be
enough. I'm not all that hungry today.'

When Bernard had gone, Maxie suddenly got frightful
stomach-ache and whimpered and wailed so much that
Otto covered his ears. But I think it would be wiser if first
of all I were to tell you in greater detail what bald Otto

had related about the mysterious Señor Lopez a few hours earlier.

*

Well, Otto was already drunk at breakfast. Full right up to the top. Perhaps he had mistaken the brandy-bottle for the coffee-pot. Or possibly he had gargled with raspberry liqueur. At any rate, he began, all unasked:

'That Lopez, he's a crazy guy. Señor means Mister. A crazy mister, that guy is. Richer than the Bank of England. On every finger two or three rings. Just give me one of them rings and I could buy the whole of Switzerland! But what would *I* do with Switzerland? Ah well, whatsomever: the fourth third at least of South America belongs to Lopez! Copper and tin and coffee beans and silver mines and haci ... haci ... haciendas with nothing but cattle, from pasture to corned beef, one, two, one, two, into the cans! Has a kind of castle down there. Between Santiago and Valparaiso. With its own airport and a hundred snipers who could shoot a cigar clean out of the hand of a common house-fly.'

That was too much for Maxie. He tittered.

'That's enough of that!' Otto growled. 'That Lopez is nothing to laugh at. It just seems so. Whenever any of these oil paintings worth a million gets swiped, it's hanging next week in his underground gallery. Could be a genuine Adolf Dürer or a Remembring or one of these modernistic painters such as the celebrated Inkasso ...'

'Picasso,' Maxie corrected him. 'And Rembrandt and Albrecht Dürer.'

'It's the same difference,' Otto said and stowed the next glass of brandy away behind his belt-buckle. 'The main thing to remember is, them pictures is hanging in his basement, Lopez's basement. Not a soul knows about them.

Not even Interpol. And even if *they* knowed about them, they couldn't do nothing. The sharp-shooters wouldn't even let them into the castle.'

'What *is* Interpol?' Maxie asked.

' 'S an abbreviation for . . . for . . . for International Police. They once very nearly got their hands on Bernard and me! When we'd lifted the gipsy fortune-teller and was waiting at Lisbon airport to fly her across in Lopez's private plane. But it worked out, in the end. She's been two years now down there in his castle laying out the cards for him every day. Like whether he should buy stocks on the Stock Exchange just then or not. Or whether he has something wrong with his liver, because I'm sorry to say he drinks like a fish and holds his liquor far too well. Or whether one of his race-horses will come in first . . .'

'And what on earth would he want with me?' Maxie asked tensely. 'Why did he want you to steal *me* this time and fly me across to him?'

Otto poured himself another glass. The bottle was almost empty. He knocked the brandy back, coughed, snuffled and said: 'The man's bored, and that's why he's collecting things. People as well as pictures. Like if they was stamps. Money's no object. He had a whole ballet troupe abducted. Lot of pretty little things they be. Have to dance something for him every evening. D'you think Lopez'll let them go? Not on your nelly. Not even when they've become grandmothers. No dice. They'd denounce him straight away. Am I right, or am I right? And he's got a famous professor locked up there as well. Because he can tell if an expensive picture's genu-ine or false.'

'And what if the professor were to deceive him?'

'He tried it on once.' Otto grinned. 'It wasn't good for his health, I can tell you. Lopez don't like to be made a fool of.'

'But *what* does he want with *me*?' Maxie asked in a trembling voice.

'Haven't the slightest. He wants you, so he'll get you, and that's that! Maybe because you're a freak. Like say a calf with two or three heads.'

Maxie stared at Otto's protuberant ears. 'A face like a pot with two handles,' he thought. And then another thought came uppermost in his mind: 'I must get away from here! Time's getting short!'

*

I've already mentioned that at this point Bernard turned up. 'We're flying on Friday,' he said and showed the flight tickets. He didn't stay long, because he wanted to lunch at 'The Loaded Dice' and relieve Otto within an hour, though the baldy didn't feel really hungry. Two portions of pickled pork with sauerkraut, he had said, would be enough for him.

'Bernard'll be coming back in an hour,' thought Maxie. 'So it's action stations! He's already got the plane tickets. It's now or never!' And so The Little Man suddenly got an acute stomach-ache and started whimpering and screaming until Otto had to put his hands over his pot-handles, I mean his ears.

If you'll promise not to repeat it to drunken Otto, I'll let you into a secret. Are you sure no one else is listening? No? Well, then, confidentially: Maxie actually had no stomach-ache! Nor was there anything wrong with his heart or his legs; he had no convulsions in his throat, nor even writer's cramp. There was obsolutely nothing wrong with him. He only pretended there was. It was all part of his plan.

'Ah-ah-ow-ow!' he groaned. 'Oh-oh-oh-oh!' he yowled. 'OO-oo-oo-ooh!' he howled, and writhed like a worm in his matchbox. 'Get a doctor!' he shrieked. 'At once! Ow-ow-ow-ow! Quickly! Quickly!'

'Where am I going to find a doctor?' Otto asked worried.

'Get a doctor!' the boy bellowed. 'Get one! Now!'

'Are you right off your rocker?' Otto cried. 'The whole city's looking for you, and here you are asking me to drag a doctor into the house and have him get us arrested.'

'Ow-ow-ow-ow!' yelled Maxie, throwing himself from side to side. 'Help! I'm dying!'

'Don't you dare!' Otto yelled back. 'That would be the last straw. Don't you do the dirty on us! There's going to be no dying here. Lopez would wring our necks if we arrived without you!' The baldy was sweating blood and tears. 'Where've you *got* this pain?'

Maxie held his stomach. 'Here!' he whimpered. 'Oh-oh-oh-oh! It's – Ow – stomach cramp! I often get it, Oo-oo-oo-oh! Quick, a doctor! Or else – Ee-ee-ee-ee! – get me some valerian drops!'

He was howling like eight hyenas at night.

'Valerian drops?' Otto groaned and wiped his handkerchief over his face. 'Where the dickens am I going to get valerian drops?'

'Chemist's!' screamed Maxie. 'Quick! Quick! Ah-ow-ow-ow!'

'But I can't leave this room just now,' cried Otto. 'Take a glass of brandy! It's medicine too.' He lifted the bottle. It was empty. 'Cor stone a crow!'

'Chemist's!' Maxie moaned. 'Otherwise I'll . . .' He sank back groaning, gasping for breath, then lay still as a log.

Otto squinted alarmed at the matchbox. He was at his wits' end. 'Have you fainted?'

'Not quite yet,' Maxie whispered. He fluttered his eyelids and made his teeth chatter a bit.

'I'll shut the door and run to a chemist's and come back in a jiffy. Right?'

'Yes.'

Otto jammed on his hat, ran out of the room, gave the key a double turn in the lock, put the key in his trouser pocket, stumbled along the corridor, flung open the door of the flat, slammed it behind him, locked it, put this second key also into his trouser pocket and staggered downstairs.

Out of the house. Through the front garden and through the iron garden gate. Looking for a chemist's. Or at least for some shop selling aspirins, and so on.

'Valerian drops for the dwarf,' he was groaning. 'And a bottle of brandy for poor old Otto.'

*

The room was locked. Until Otto returned, no one could enter and no one could get out. Not even Maxie could get out. But that was no longer necessary.

Eh? *Why* was that no longer necessary? Don't you know why? Surely you must have guessed already? No? Well, then, listen! It was no longer necessary, quite simply because Maxie was no longer in the room. He had left it at the same time as Otto. But how? On Otto's back of course! That was the plan which he had thought out for himself.

The Little Man had never believed that Otto would bring a doctor. Not for one second. But this was part of his plan. The baldy would much rather run to a chemist's, Maxie had reasoned. And that was exactly what had happened.

When Otto had taken his hat from the peg, he had turned his back on the matchbox – and at once Maxie, making a soundless leap, had landed on Otto's jacket and climbed up. For a famous artiste this was child's play.

And while Otto had been locking the room door and
the flat door and going down the stairs and out of the
house and running through the front garden, Maxie had
all the time been clinging to Otto's shoulder.

On reaching the garden gate Maxie had jumped across
to one of the iron bars. Not a hitch. Training tells.

His forehead hurt a little. Cast-iron is not india-rubber.
Probably he would have a bruise or a bump or even both.
No matter!

Maxie was now sitting on one of the two high stone
posts on either side of the garden gate, each one of which
was topped by a stone ball. He sat up there and took a

deep breath. The air smelt of jasmine. And it smelt of freedom, too!

Maxie was in raptures. But this was not the right time for jasmine and raptures. He must get away from here. He must push on. Otto would not be away for long. In less than an hour Bernard would come back from 'The Loaded Dice'! Every minute was as precious as a whole year in more peaceful times.

The street was empty, as if there were no more people left on earth. The houses on the other side stood silent, like houses of the dead.

Maxie turned round and looked up at the door of the house through which, shortly before, Otto had stumbled out bearing him on his shoulder. Next to the door hung a blue plate with a white number on it. And under the number stood, in small white letters, the name of the street.

'Kickelhahnstrasse 12,' Maxie murmured. '12 Kickelhahn Street.' Just as he was saying it to himself for the third time, a window opened on the ground floor of a house opposite. Then a boy came and lolled out over the window-ledge, took a brown paperbag of cherries out of his pocket and started putting one cherry after another in his mouth and spitting the stones out into the street. He was aiming at a small green children's ball lying around outside, and wasn't doing at all badly.

20

The cherry-stone-spitter gets angry and is called Jakob. Maxie makes a telephone call and waits for whatever the future may bring. Cars 1, 2 and 3. Bald Otto rides in a car. Maxie rides in a car. Jakob rides in a car. The quiet street is quiet again.

'HELLO, there!' Maxie called.

But the boy at the window took no notice and went on practising his shots. It was not all that easy to hit the green ball with a cherry-stone. Sailors maybe could have done it. (As every child knows, those chaps must be champion spitters. As helmsman and captain they leave something to be desired. Probably it's a question of age.)

'Hello, there!' Maxie called even louder.

The boy glanced across the street, but as he could see no one he went on carefully spitting out stones.

Maxie was getting uneasy. Time was passing. What could he do? How could he make the boy get a move on? Fortunately he got an idea which promised to be very successful. 'I'll call him names all the time,' he thought, 'until he really begins to see red.'

So again he shouted 'Halloooh!' and then, as the boy did not react, but simply stuck another cherry in his mouth, cried: 'Are you deaf, you old blockhead?'

The boy started, accidentally swallowing a cherry-stone and stared grimly in Maxie's direction. Where was the blighter with that cheeky voice?

'Don't be such a sissy!' Maxie bellowed. 'Or your parents'll take you back to be changed at the next sales.'

At that, the boy swung his legs over the window-ledge. 'That's going a bit too far,' he blurted out. 'A joke's a joke!' He hopped down to the pavement, came tearing across the street, stopped in front of the garden gate, doubled his fists aggressively and couldn't see a soul anywhere. 'Come out, you coward!' he yelled, beside himself. 'Come out, of the bushes, you swine! I'll squash you between the palms of my hands!'

Maxie had to laugh at that.

The boy raised his head, discovered Maxie leaning against the stone ball on the top of the pillar, and gaped flabbergasted at him. He was going to say something but he had been deprived of speech. He couldn't utter a sound.

'Do you know who I am?' Maxie asked.

The boy nodded eagerly.

'Will you help me?'

The boy nodded even more eagerly. His eyes were sparkling.

'I *had* to annoy you like that,' Maxie explained, 'otherwise you'd never have come across. Sorry.'

The boy nodded again. Or rather, he was just about to nod. Because he finally managed to say something: 'Don't mention it, Little Man,' he said. 'Let's forget it. My name is Jakob.'

'I'm called Maxie. Have you a telephone?'

151

Jakob nodded.

'Hold your hand up!' Maxie commanded. 'But mind you don't squash me between the palms of your hands.'

Jakob blushed deep red but held his hand as high as he could. Maxie jumped down from the pillar. Right into the middle of the open hand.

Jakob dashed across the street, set The Little Man on the window-ledge, climbed the wall and swung himself into the room. Then he took hold of Maxie again and ran to a desk. A telephone was standing on it.

'Whom do you want to call?' Jakob asked.

'The Criminal Investigation Bureau,' said Maxie. 'Because if I call Hokus at the hotel – but you don't know Hokus.'

'Excuse me!' replied Jakob. 'Of course I know Professor Hokus von Pokus. I know both of you. Through the circus and TV and newspapers and everything.'

'Because if I call Hokus he'll come at once and wring bald Otto's neck. And then Bernard's. That would only complicate matters.'

'I've got you,' Jakob said. 'Otto and Bernard are the kidnappers.' He looked at a newspaper-cutting sticking in the blotter. 'Here is the police message. With their telephone number and all.'

'Jolly good, Jakob,' said Maxie, and once again rubbed his hands for glee. 'As soon as you've got someone on the line, lay the receiver on the desk, will you? Then I can talk to them myself.'

Jakob dialled the telephone number and said after a while: 'Please connect me with Detective Inspector Steinbiss! He's busy? That's a pity. Well, give him The Little Man's very best wishes!' Jakob grinned at Maxie and murmured: 'That shook him. The cop nearly had a stroke!'

Three seconds later a voice boomed out of the telephone; it sounded as if the detective were standing right in the middle of the room. 'Steinbiss here! What *is* it?'

Maxie knelt in front of the mouthpiece and shouted: 'This is The Little Man speaking! Maxie Pichelsteiner! I've escaped! From house number 12 Kickelhahn Street. Otto will be back soon. Now I'm in the house opposite . . .'

'Number 17,' Jakob hurriedly whispered. 'Name Hurtig. Ground floor left.'

'House number 17, name Hurtig, ground floor left. D'you understand? Just a tick, I must dash to the earpiece.'

Maxie ran to the earpiece.

'We'll be with you straight away,' the Detective Inspector said. 'Meanwhile, be careful! Anything else?'

Maxie leaped back to the mouthpiece and in his excitement almost stuck his head into it: 'Please don't use your sirens and warning lights. Otto is still at the chemist's and would smell a rat! And the most important thing, Defective Injector, I mean Dejected Infector, I mean . . .

Oh, I'm all mixed up! *Don't* say anything to Hokus! Not yet, not yet! Please, please, and please once again! He gets so easily worked up. Is he all right? And Rosa Marzipan too? And . . .'

Jakob held the receiver to his ear and signed to Maxie that they'd been cut off. 'All quiet on the western front. Probably the valiant officers of the law have just jumped from the third storey straight into their patrol cars. With twenty pistols in their holsters.'

'More haste, less speed,' Maxie said. 'Please carry me to the window!'

Jakob laid the telephone receiver back on the rest. 'It will be a great honour for me, Herr von Pichelsteiner.'

*

They sat at the open window and waited impatiently for whatever the future would bring. Who would be the first to reach the post? Detective Inspector Steinbiss and his men? Or bald Otto with the valerian drops?

Jakob was again spitting cherry-stones at the green ball and still hadn't quite got his range. 'Spitting at a target is difficult,' he stated. 'Almost as difficult as life itself.'

'And why is life more difficult?' Maxie asked.

'My dear sir!' The other boy sighed. 'It's a sad look-out. Father away. Mother away. Son feeding himself on fruit. What could be worse?'

'When did they abandon you?' Maxie asked, deeply shocked.

'Early this morning.'

'For good?'

'Not altogether. They'll be back tomorrow evening.'

They both burst out laughing.

'Aunt Anna,' Jakob informed Maxie, 'has had her leg bitten by a stork. I couldn't talk my parents out of it. They simply had to see the stork or the bite in her leg or the baby.'

'And they left only a bag of cherries here for you?'

'Heaven forbid!' Jakob said in insulted tones. 'I had enough cash to fill three money-boxes. Was to have eaten at restaurants. At lunchtime and this evening and tomorrow lunchtime. But . . .'

'But what?'

'As I was going into school, I saw Fritz Griebitz standing outside crying. Carrying his little dachshund in his arms, that always went with him to the school gates and then back home. He had been run over by a motor-car. He was called Puffi.'

'Oh,' Maxie murmured.

'So we collected some money. For the funeral and for Puffi number two. And when we got into the classroom, the teacher looked at the clock. Boy, did he give us a sour look! And there was Fritz howling his eyes out . . . and the dead dachshund at the porter's lodge . . . and only a few coppers left until tomorrow evening . . . and nothing but cherries . . . Now, is life difficult, or isn't it?'

Maxie nodded understandingly. He was nibbling and gnawing at a cherry which he was holding in both hands. It looked as if he were trying to lift a giant pumpkin that had won the Gold Medal at the World Fair. And he said: 'Hold on a little longer, Jakob, and we'll both be eating pineapple tart.'

'Fruit again!' said Jakob despondently.

*

Detective Inspector Steinbiss and Inspector Müller came walking rapidly along Kickelhahn Street. Three cars with the rest of the men were waiting, just round the corner, in Three Stars Lane.

'That's number 12 over there,' the Inspector murmured. 'That's where he was held prisoner.'

'Very quiet street,' the Detective Inspector said. Then he grabbed his cheek. 'Who's that shooting cherry-stones?'

'Excuse me, sir,' a boy shouted. 'I was trying to hit that green ball.'

'Since when do I look like a green ball?' the Detective Inspector grumbled.

'Number 17, ground floor left,' Inspector Müller whispered. 'This is it.'

The Detective Inspector went to the open window. 'Are you called Hurtig by any chance?'

'Hurtig, that's right,' Jakob replied. 'But certainly not "by any chance".'

Inspector Müller grinned.

'Criminal Investigation Bureau!' the Inspector grunted. 'We've come to get The Little Man.'

Jakob said: 'A lot of people would like to do that. May I see your identification cards?'

At first Herr Steinbiss's fingers twitched convulsively. But then he pulled out his identification card and showed it to the cheeky little monkey.

Jakob studied the card thoroughly. 'These are the right ones, Maxie,' he said.

Only then did Maxie raise his head above the window-ledge. 'How d'ye do, gentlemen! How is he?'

'Who?'

'Hokus, of course!'

'He's well on the way to being a professional starving man,' the detective said drily.

Maxie's face darkened. But only for a second. Then he was radiant again, and rubbed his hands. 'This evening he's going to eat at least four veal cutlets. I'm looking forward to seeing it already!'

Suddenly they heard hurried, tipsy footsteps!

Maxie climbed on the window-ledge. 'That's bald Otto,' he whispered.

Otto was coming along on the other side with rather uncertain, drunken steps, holding a big fat bottle clasped to his breast.

'Is that full of valerian drops?' Jakob asked in astonishment.

Maxie giggled. 'That's brandy! His bottle was empty. That's why he ran so fast to the chemist's.'

'Well now, let's get cracking,' Herr Steinbiss said to Herr Müller.

'One moment!' Maxie whispered. Then he jumped on the Detective Inspector's sleeve and in a trice had climbed into his breast pocket.

Otto was just going to turn into the garden gate of Number 12 when they barred his way. 'What's up?' he asked furiously, and gave the two men a nasty look.

'Criminal Investigation Bureau,' the Detective Inspector said. 'You are under arrest.'

'Oh-oh! You don't say so!' Otto mocked, and turned to run away.

But Herr Müller was too fast for him. He tackled Otto firmly. 'Ow!' yelled Otto and let his big bottle fall. It smashed. Herr Steinbiss blew on his policeman's whistle. Three cars came out of Three Stars Lane and braked. Six plain-clothes officers jumped out on the pavement.

'Patrol car number one will take the arrested man at once to the police station,' the Detective Inspector ordered. 'The Inspector will take the men from patrol car number two and search the house and the flat.'

'First floor on the left,' said Maxie. 'Otto has the keys in his right-hand trouser pocket.' And at once an officer was fishing out the keys.

Bald Otto blinked, as if struck by lightning, at the Detective Inspector's breast pocket. Then he bellowed: 'You little good-for-nothing! How did you get out ...' But before he could bawl out the end of his sentence, he was sitting, under strong guard, in patrol car number one, which immediately drove away.

An officer from car number two announced: 'Detective Inspector Steinbiss, sir! The police radio informed us two minutes ago that house number 12 in Kickelhahn Street belongs to a South American trading company.'

'I'm not at all surprised,' Maxie remarked. 'It all adds up, Señor Lopez and everything.'

158

Inspector Müller asked in amazement: 'What do *you* know about Lopez?'

'Not much,' replied The Little Man. 'But too much to tell you now.'

Herr Steinbiss nodded brusquely. 'He's right. We're in a hurry. Car number two, take over the house. Car number three will take me and Maxie to the Professor at his hotel.'

'No,' said Maxie. 'We must first go to "The Loaded Dice" and arrest Bernard while he's having lunch. He's ten times worse than bald Otto. It was he who was the false waiter in the white jacket!'

The Detective Inspector couldn't help laughing. 'Maxie's in charge, Maxie knows everything. Let's get going, car number three, to "The Loaded Dice"!' He shoved himself into the seat next to the driver and felt for his revolver.

'One moment!' Maxie suddenly cried and leaned right out of the breast pocket. 'Car number two must please bring my matchbox with them! Otherwise I'll have to sleep in my awful "heavenly bed" tonight.'

'That would be really dreadful,' said Inspector Müller as he stormed into the house with his men.

'What are we waiting for?' the Detective Inspector asked the driver of car number three. 'Let's get going!'

'I can't get going,' the driver informed him. 'There's a boy standing on the running-board.'

Jakob was looking through the car window. 'Am I invited to have some pineapple tart or not?'

Maxie heaved a sigh, as if it were his very last, or at least the one before the very last. 'I should be heartily ashamed of myself,' he stammered. 'I've barely got myself out of this mess, and already I'm forgetting my best friends!'

Jakob Hurtig quickly got into the car. 'Don't give it a thought, man!'

Patrol car number one was on its way to the police station with bald Otto. Patrol car number three was now racing towards 'The Loaded Dice'. Patrol car number two was standing in front of house number 12. Kickelhahn Street and the green ball were again lying as quiet as they had been half an hour ago.

On the pavement there glittered the fragments of a brandy bottle. Otherwise, it seemed, nothing had changed.

21

Uproar in 'The Loaded Dice'. Jakob
would rather have had a 'knuckles-of-
veal' hotel. Tears and training. Marzipan with goose-flesh. Strong mustard.
Who gets the reward? Maxie mimics
bald Otto. What's the smallest five-
figure sum?

'The Loaded Dice' was not much of a place, but the grub
was good. I've nothing against that. If the soup is real
meat broth, the plate doesn't have to be of genuine porcelain. Usually it's the other way round.

The customers sat and ate at well-scrubbed tables, and
they enjoyed their food. Only today, Bernard pulled a
face. The strapping proprietress, bringing him his dessert,
noticed this at once. 'So it don't taste good again?' she
asked grimly.

'High time I go somewhere people know how to cook,'
he retorted.

'High time you don't come back to my place,' she snapped and snatched the dessert away from under his nose. (By
the way, it was caramel pudding with raspberry sauce.)

'Bring back that daft shivery-shaky stuff!' he ordered icily. You know what his refrigerator voice was like!

'I'd be obliged if you was to get out of my caff double quick!' she calmly gave answer. 'The two portions pickled pork is being kept for your bald mate. That's the lot. As for *you* – git out! I don't want no money. Kindly consider yourself my guest and scram! Go on, beat it, you horrible old vulture you!'

Bernard grabbed at the plate in his rage.

But the proprietress stepped back and threw the whole thing right in his face.

Whether one likes caramel pudding with raspberry sauce is a matter of personal preference. I, for example don't like it. But – plonk right in your face? Nobody likes it served *that* way. Nevertheless Bernard stuck out his tongue and eagerly lapped up the raspberry sauce trickling down his face. He was afraid it would stain his white shirt and light-grey suit and smart necktie.

The actual pudding – a really excellent pudding – stuck in his hair and gummed up his ice-blue eyes. He groped with all ten fingers in the air and over his face, felt for the napkin, tried to find his handkerchief in his trouser pocket – and all this naturally didn't make things any better.

The customers were laughing. The proprietress was laughing. And when a little girl at the next table cried: 'Mummy, the man looks like a pig!' then the general merriment knew no bounds.

Yet all of a sudden they were all as still as mice. What had happened?

Bernard squinted through the clammy caramel pudding and gave a start: he had every reason to. For three men were standing round him and seemed to be finding him not funny at all.

162

The worst thing was that out of one of the men's breast pockets leaned a familiar little figure, who pointed to Bernard and stated, loud and clear: 'Detective Inspector, that's him!'

*

After they had delivered Bernard, still all gummed-up, to the police station, Maxie was to be driven back to his hotel. Jakob Hurtig, who was standing beside the car, declared: 'I don't want to disturb you any longer.'

'You're coming with me!' said Maxie. 'For the pineapple tart and everything.'

'Of course you're coming with us!' the Detective Inspector said. 'After all, I have to write down your personal details and everything.'

'That's O.K. by me,' Jakob replied. 'After all, my parents are at Aunt Anna's seeing to the stork and everything.'

Then the three of them laughed and were driven speedily back to the hotel.

*

Inspector Müller had telephoned beforehand. And so the entire staff was there, from the manager to the pages and liftboys, all waiting in the lobby to shout: 'Long shall he live! Long shall he live! Three cheers!' The telephone operators were waving huge sheaves of flowers in the air. And the pastry chef presented Maxie with a pineapple tart. It was as big as the spare wheel of a long-distance lorry.

'There now, what did I tell you?' The Little Man said to Jakob. 'Pineapple tart!'

Jakob pulled a face. 'Don't they have anything else

here? Is this a pineapple-tart hotel? I'd definitely prefer a knuckles-of-veal hotel.'

Maxie beckoned to the manager. 'Have you any knuckles of veal today?'

'At least three dozen,' the manager said. 'Tender as butter.'

'How many do you want?' Maxie asked.

'One will do,' said Jakob. 'If possible, with potato salad.'

'Very well. One knuckle of veal with potato salad.'

'Very well. One knuckle of veal with potato salad for the young gentleman,' the manager repeated the order.

'No, no!' said Jakob. 'For *me*!'

Rosa Marzipan went up in the lift with Maxie. She held The Little Man firmly in both hands and pressed his face gently against her marzipan cheek.

'Does he know?' Maxie asked.

She nodded. 'Five minutes ago. But he didn't want to come down into the lobby.'

The lift stopped. Rosa went along the corridor and knocked. 'Here we are!'

The door opened. The Professor spread wide both his arms and cried: 'Come in, both of you!' He sounded as if he had a cold in the nose.

Rosa smiled and shook her head. 'I don't like to see men weeping. I'll come back for you in an hour.' Then she carefully placed The Little Man in Hokus's hand, dropped a deep curtsy and ran back to the lift. She was gone.

*

When she laid her ear to the door an hour later, that ear got a big surprise. There was no longer any trace of weeping to be heard. Instead, Rosa heard cries of command! And as she cautiously opened the door she saw Maxie scrambling about on Winsome Waldemar. He was training fit to beat the band!

'Faster, my boy!' Hokus ordered him. 'More smoothly! Oh, you've got fat! You must get rid of that pot-belly. What must you get rid of?'

'My bot-belly!'

'What must you get rid of?'

'My pot-belly!' Maxie chortled and disappeared inside Waldemar's necktie. Soon he had loosened the knot and Maxie, guided unfailingly by Hokus's hand, slithered with the tie down into the latter's left pocket.

Winsome Waldemar went on staring steadily ahead and had noticed nothing. Rosa peeped through the open door and saw nothing either. 'Hooray, the artistes!' she cried and clapped her hands. Emma and Minna, the two doves, were hopping backwards and forwards along the top of the wardrobe, fluttering their wings with excitement.

'Two more training sessions, and he'll be fit.' Hokus said in a satisfied voice. 'We can perform again on Friday.'

Maxie popped his head out of the Professor's pocket, like a jack-in-the-box. 'That's impossible, Your Honour! On Friday I'm flying to join Señor Lopez in South America with bald Otto and pudding-face Bernard.'

'What desperate-sounding names!' cried Rosa. 'They give me goose-flesh all over.'

165

Maxie rubbed his hands. 'Show me! Marzipan with goose-flesh all over is something I'd very much like to see, just once.'

Rosa winked at Hokus. 'Life in the criminal fraternity unfortunately seems to have rubbed off on Herr Pichelsteiner somewhat. He's become frivolous.'

Hokus fished Maxie out of his pocket. 'I'll put him in King Bileam's bath. Cleanliness is next to godliness.'

*

They had dinner in the Blue Saloon and it went off to everyone's satisfaction, even Jakob's. Though when he got his veal knuckles tears came into his eyes. But this was caused only by the strong English mustard which he was tasting for the first time. 'We live and learn,' he said, wafting cool air with his napkin into his open mouth.

Hokus did not eat four veal cutlets, only two. And even that took time. For there were so many things to talk about: for example, with Herr Brausewetter about the circus performance on Friday; at intervals with the reporters outside the dining-room and on the telephone; and not least with Detective Inspector Steinbiss, who, late though it was, came over from the police station.

The others were already eating their dessert. 'Oh, pineapple tarts!' he cried enthusiastically. 'My favourite dish!' And then he polished off three immensely big portions.

Maxie and Jakob thought that was very comical. But they soon became serious again. For Hokus asked the Detective Inspector during his second piece of pineapple tart: 'Now who is actually the person to receive the reward I offered?'

'Jakob!' Maxie cried. 'It's as clear as day!'

'Me? Why me?' Jakob spoke up. 'Certainly not! If Maxie had not teased me in so beastly a way, I should still be sitting at the window, same as before, unaware of anything. You might just as well give your money to bald Otto in jail. For after all, it was *he* who freed Maxie.'

'Yes, but without knowing he was doing so,' Herr Brausewetter stated. 'He intended to buy valerian drops, that was all.'

'And what did I intend to do?' Jakob Hurtig asked. 'I only intended to punch some big-mouth on the nose.'

'And squash him between the palms of your hands!' Maxie cried, laughing. He was sitting on the table and allowing Rosa to feed him with bits of pineapple tart.

'Another little morsel?' she asked.

He shook his head. 'No, thank you. All I want now is a little marzipan with goose-flesh.'

She wagged the cake-fork at him. 'That's not for little boys.'

'Oh, I know,' he teased. 'You're keeping it all for Hokus.'

Then Rosa blushed. But no one saw it except Maxie.

For the Detective Inspector was already shoving back his plate and saying briskly: 'It was thanks to The Little Man himself that he was not abducted abroad. He was at one and the same time the missing person and the finder. If anyone can prove the contrary to me, then I'm a dustman.'

Well, the others did not want to have any part in bringing about such a drastic change of occupation. And therefore nobody spoke, and the party went on as merrily as ever. Maxie stole the show. He mimicked bald Otto, staggered about the table between the plates and cups, and at the same time related most of what that drunken old rascal Otto had told him about Señor Lopez, the castle in South America, the underground art gallery, the gypsy fortune-teller, the bodyguard of snipers and the poor ballet dancers.

The only person who did not laugh outright at Maxie's masterly performance, but only occasionally grinned, was Detective Inspector Steinbiss. He took down in shorthand everything The Little Man uttered. Then he slammed his notebook shut and made a hurried departure. 'I must spend a few more hours questioning the two villains,' he said.

'Even Interpol is helpless where Lopez is concerned!' Maxie shouted after him. 'The fellow's much too rich!'

The Detective Inspector, who had already reached the door, started and turned round. 'He's little, but oh-oh . . .' he said appreciatively. 'What about it? Would you like to be my assistant?'

Maxie gave him a gracious bow. 'No, thank you, Detective Inspector. I am, and shall always remain, an artiste.'

*

When Jakob Hurtig was hurtling into bed that night he tossed his jacket over a chair and heard the sound of paper rustling in the inside pocket. There he discovered an open cheque made out in his name, read the amount, whispered 'Holy Moses!' and sat down on the edge of the bed.

There was also a note. It read: 'Dear Jakob, heartiest thanks for your help. Your new friends Maxie and Hokus.' It was a five-figure amount. And if it had been only the smallest five-figure sum, it would still have been a lot of money for a boy whose father was area representative for a built-in furniture company.

(Incidentally: what *is* the smallest possible five-figure sum?)

*

When Hokus came back with Maxie into their hotel room, the good old matchbox was lying there on the bedside table. And under the cover lay a note. It read:

Dear Little Man,
    Herewith as per orders your heavenly bed from Kickelhahn Street.

MÜLLER
Police Inspector

Maxie rubbed his hands and said: 'Now I have all I want.'

22

Why the Gala Performance lasted twenty-seven minutes longer. Herr Brausewetter reads out three telegrams. Jakob temporarily loses his temper. The police take a bow. Entry of the chief characters. Rejoicing without end. END.

ON Friday, of course, Ringmaster Brausewetter was really in his element. Once more an evening after his own heart! He would have liked to pull on three snow-white pairs of kid gloves one over the other, and to wear two top-hats! It was in any case a Gala Performance that was well worth seeing. He understood that kind of thing, did our Ringmaster Brausewetter, Donnerbrausewetter rather! (Or do you like 'Brausedonnerwetter' better?)

The programme lasted twenty-seven minutes longer than usual, but this was not the fault of the lions or the elephants or the artistes. They all performed with their usual precision. There were two reasons.

Firstly, Ringmaster Brausewetter read out a few of the most important telegrams of congratulation that Maxie had received. I can still remember three of them very well.

The Gymnastic Association in Pichelstein had wired:

MAXIE PICHELSTEINER
STILKE'S CIRCUS
BERLIN
GREETINGS AND BLESSINGS WE WERE STANDING VIGI-
LANTLY IN STANDING-IN POSITION AS FOR A GRAND
CIRCLE WITH SPLITS FINISH STOP BRAVO STOP ARE
PROUD OF YOU STOP
        ALL PICHELSTEINERS IN PICHELSTEIN

The second telegram had come from the Kingdom of
Breganzona. It made a deep impression in the audience.
Because there are not many kings left nowadays. So one
must make the most of them and be thankful for any sign
of life. The telegram read:

from III BREGANZONA K 1435
        MAXIE PICHELSTEINER
        STILKE'S CIRCUS BERLIN =
WERE FRIGHTFULLY WORKED UP STOP FIRST WITH
WORRY NOW WITH JOY STOP SAFETY CHAIN FOR HOTEL
ROOM DOOR FOLLOWS EXPRESS AIRMAIL STOP COME
AND VISIT US IN BREGANZONA STOP NICE CASTLE NICE
PEOPLE STOP OUR GREETINGS ALSO TO PROFESSOR
HOKUS STOP =
YOUR KING BILEAM AND ALL HIS FAMILY AND PEOPLE +

The third cable I remember came from Hollywood.
The film company which I have already mentioned
cabled this:

from 1495 HOLLYWOOD F 34/36 87 =
        LITTLE MAN
        STILKE'S CIRCUS BERLIN
CONGRATULATIONS ON KIDNAPPING AND SELF RESCUE
STOP BRILLIANTLY SUITED TO MOVIE STOP DRAFT CON-
TRACT ON THE WAY STOP EUROPEAN REPRESENTATIVE
WITH CARTE BLANCHE ARRIVING MONDAY = +

Secondly, before the entrance of Maxie and Hokus,

171

Ringmaster Brausewetter introduced the evening's guests of honour who were sitting in three special boxes illuminated by spot-lights.

First of all the schoolboy Jakob Hurtig: he responded to the applause by shaking his clasped hands above his head and bowing in all directions from the waist. Like a champion boxer who has just knocked out some dreaded battering-ram from Winnesota.

Then Jakob sat down proudly again between his parents. 'Sit up straight!' his mother hissed at him and gave him a smack between the shoulder-blades. (You know the sort of thing!)

Jakob's face darkened. He jerked away from her and whispered to his father: 'Your spouse is unfortunately poisoning the one day of glory of your son who has recently come into a lot of money. Do you consider this proper or improper?'

The elder Hurtig bit his lips. He much admired Jakob's ornate style. And he really couldn't think of an answer. For there was already another burst of applause, because Ringmaster Brausewetter was introducing the crews of the three patrol cars, then Inspector Müller, and finally Detective Inspector Steinbiss in person.

Scarcely had the applause died away than the next incident broke out. A group of young people started bellowing for all they were worth: 'We want bald Otto! We want pudding-face Bernard! We want the dirty dogs!' And because all the spectators had read the newspapers and listened to the radio, the whole Big Top shuddered with gales of laughter. It was capital fun. Because everybody well knew that Otto and Bernard could not be presented in the circus ring because they were behind bars!

Suddenly Ringmaster Brausewetter made a compelling gesture. And there was sudden stillness, as at the eye of a typhoon. Everyone knew what would be coming next and who would be coming next. You might have heard a pin drop, if a pin had dropped. But no pin dropped.

'And now, ladies and gentlemen!' called Ringmaster Brausewetter, 'now at last you are about to see once more, to welcome back and to gaze in wonder at your and our and everybody's darling, he who is the littlest biggest hero in criminal history, he who is the biggest littlest artiste in the circus firmament, he and his paternal mentor Hokus von Pokus, the Professor and Past Master of Applied Magic! Your applause, I already know, will be unprecedented. I ask you not to worry! Anyone who breaks his hands may apply to the box office at the end of the performance for a new pair!'

Brausewetter shot his right arm vertically into the air. Like a cavalry general giving the signal for a cavalry charge. Then he galloped, though not on a horse, out of the circus ring.

The orchestra played a deafening fanfare, using all its drums and brass!

And in the entrance to the ring there appeared, immaculate and elegant as ever, Professor Hokus von Pokus. On his outstretched hand stood Maxie, waving and smiling in every direction. But what more is there for me to say? Unlike this book, the rejoicing went on without

END

If you have enjoyed this book and would like to know about others which we publish, why not join the Puffin Club? You will receive the club magazine, *Puffin Post*, four times a year and a smart badge and membership book. You will also be able to enter all competitions. For details of cost and an application form send a stamped addressed envelope to:

The Puffin Club, Dept. A
Penguin Books Limited
Bath Road
Harmondsworth
Middlesex